GREETINGS!

MY NAME IS B.O.R.T.R.O.N. AND FOR CENTURIES MY CREWS AND I HAVE TRAVELED THE GLOBE TO SAVE LIVES AND PROPERTY.

SOME PEOPLE THINK I'M A SPACESHIP, BUT ACTUALLY I AM AN ACCELERATED SPEED AND DISTANCE (ASD) TRANSPORTER. WHAT DOES THAT MEAN?, YOU MAY BE WONDERING. WELL, IF YOU CAN IMAGINE TRAVELING TO THE OTHER SIDE OF THE WORLD IN THE BLINK OF AN EYE AND ENTERING AN ALTERED TIME ZONE THAT ALLOWS YOU TO ACCOMPLISH ASTONISHING THINGS IN THE EQUIVALENT OF MINUTES AT HOME, THEN YOU'VE GOT IT!

JOIN CLUB US ON THIS MISSION TO EGYPT WHERE THEY MUST STOP THIEVES FROM ROBBING A TOMB FOR A METAL THAT WILL KILL THOUSANDS OF PEOPLE. IT'S A THRILL A MINUTE, AND YOU CAN BE A PART OF IT BY JUST TURNING THE PAGE.

BUCKLE UP AND GET READY FOR THE RIDE OF YOUR LIFE!

CLUB US
by Mya Reyes

Published by ValMar Publishing
Las Vegas, NV 89145 USA

www.ValMarPublishing.com

© 2021 Mya Reyes
All rights reserved. No portion of this book may be reproduced in any form without permission from the publisher, except as permitted by U.S. copyright law.

For permissions contact:
info@ValMarPublishing.com

Cover illustration by Claudia Gadotti
Graphics by Kate Z. Stone & Jake Naylor
Arabic translations by Iman Haggag

ISBN: 978-1-955079-04-4

EVIL IN EGYPT

Mya Reyes

CLUB US
THE SERIES

The first book in the CLUB US series, **PERIL IN PARIS** is the proud recipient of the Moonbeam Pre-Teen Mystery Silver Award. It was also named a Winner in the Royal Dragonfly Book Awards.

ENJOY THE EXCITEMENT OF THE FULL SERIES:

Peril in Paris
Crisis in Cuba
Intrigue in Italy
Evil in Egypt
Mayhem in Mexico
Anguish in Australia
Menace in Morocco
Greed in Greece
Threat in Thailand
Long Shot in London
Bravery in Brazil
Chaos in Canada
Terror in Tanzania

*To all the kids who will make our world
a better place to live.*

Here's what they're saying!

"I really like reading the CLUB US books. I never thought they would be so interesting and fun!"
— Henna, age 12

"I laugh a lot when I read these books and I really like learning the different languages."
— Will, age 9

"I don't know which one of the books I like the best. They are all cool and exciting!"
— Mike, age 11

"My family went to Paris once and it was just like in the book. I hope one day we can go to some of the other countries that the CLUB US kids visit."
—Gabe, age 10

"This book is a complete page-turner, so many exciting twists and turns. If your kids are looking for a great series, full of adventure and fun, look no further!"
—Kenadie Richardson, English Teacher

"When I was reading the book about Cuba, I imagined myself diving under water with all the beautiful fish. I hope one day I'll be able to go there and do all the fun things the kids in the book did, especially being in the Carnival!"
— Madisen, age1

EVIL IN EGYPT

Mya Reyes

Cover illustration by Claudia Gadotti
Graphics by Kate Z. Stone and Jake Naylor

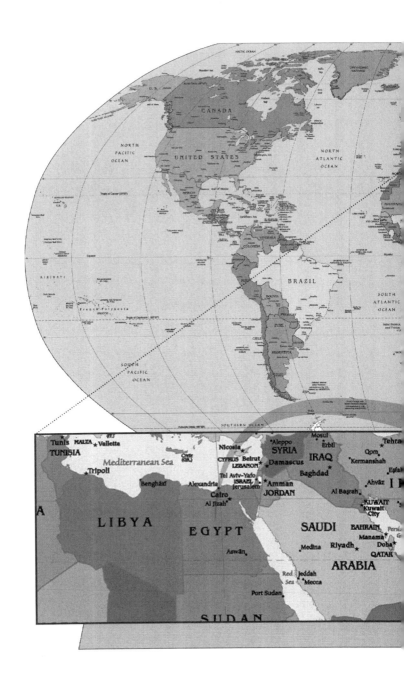

FUN FACTS ABOUT ANCIENT EGYPT:

- Men and women wore makeup as they thought it had healing powers.
- Their scientists invented medicine, paper, pens, and even toothpaste!
- Many Gods and Goddesses had a human body and an animal head.
- They played board games especially Senet, a game similar to chess.
- The Egyptian civilization was the first to keep domesticated pets.

YOU CAN JOIN CLUB US!

IT'S FREE!

AS A MEMBER YOU WILL HAVE ACCESS TO DOWNLOAD OR RECEIVE:

- A VIP Membership card
- A CLUB US Passport
- Printable country stamps to add to your passport
- Entry into fun contests
- Newsletters with CLUB US updates and activities
- Access to printables and games
- A sneak peek at upcoming books in the Club Us series

It's easy! Just ask your parent to visit www.clubus.us with you to learn more and sign up!

OUR TEAM

GOLD

NIKKO

KIAN

CASSIE

EDDIE

MR. SMITH

BARKS

KEEP IN MIND!

When reading CLUB US adventures, you will also learn the language of the countries where the missions take place. When you see a word in the other language, turn to the Glossary in the back of the book to learn the pronunciation and definition.

THE ADVENTURE BEGINS NOW!

CHAPTER 1

(واحد)
~ <u>wa</u>-heed ~

Mr. Smith had pep in his step today. He grabbed his hat and cane from the entry, closed the front door behind him, and briskly walked out to the sidewalk. Turning right, he stopped to enjoy a deep breath of fresh summer air. Even through his shaded sunglasses, the sun shone brighter, the flowers were more colorful, and the air was full of happy sounds.

Everything seemed different, but even he knew the only thing that had changed was him. In recent years the old man had lived a very lonely life. Ever since he lost his wife and only son, Jimmy, in a terrible car accident, he had closed himself off to the rest of the world.

With no one to talk to, enjoy fun activities with, and celebrate life's milestones, he began to feel more and more hopeless. His daily routine of breakfast, game shows, lunch, game shows, dinner, nightly news, and bedtime was so predictable that even the birds in his garden knew when it was time to go to sleep.

Since getting to know the CLUB US crew—Gold, Eddie, Cassie, Nikko, and Kian—Mr. Smith felt himself returning to the happy man he had once been. The relationships he developed with the kids had given his life meaning again and he was grateful. Though the kids would never realize it, their friendship was the most important thing in Mr. Smith's life and made living worthwhile again.

Tomorrow was the Fourth of July, and he had

invited the kids, and their families, to join him for a picnic in his backyard. He loved cooking and had done very little of it since Elizabeth was no longer around. For the past week he had gone through the great recipes they had prepared together and had planned a very special day for his new friends.

He was eager to see Gold and Eddie's parents again, as well as Cassie's dad, John. He even wondered what her sister was like now. As a teenager, Carla was part of a generation that he knew nothing about. Was it Gen X? Y? Z? He had no idea and wanted to spend some time with her to find out.

Mr. Smith hadn't met Kian's nor Nikko's families and was looking forward to it. He crossed his fingers that they would all like the meal he prepared and hoped the day would be as special as he imagined.

"Hi, James!" said a lady with white hair as she walked toward him.

"Hi," said Mr. Smith with a smile. He wasn't sure if he knew her, but he wanted to be friendly.

"I haven't seen you for years. You remember me, don't you? Jannie Hockenhull."

"Of course, I do, Jannie." And he did. She was one of Elizabeth's friends, and he remembered her kind smile from the times she visited with his wife at home.

"How have you been?" he asked.

"Oh, I'm doing great, Just getting old is all," she said with a laugh.

"Ha! Aren't we all?" chucked Mr. Smith.

"It's great seeing you again, James." She gave him a hug, and a sincere look that told him how sorry she was that Elizabeth had passed.

"Same here, Jannie."

He hadn't seen any of his old friends for a very long time. He knew that being with them would bring back memories of his beautiful wife and son, and he wasn't sure if he could hold himself together. Seeing Jannie was good. Yes, it made him think of Elizabeth, but with happiness and appreciation for the good times they shared. He realized he was a lucky man and had memories that would always bring him joy.

"Hi, Mr. Smith," said a young lady. She waved and hurried by as she talked on her cell phone. Before he could respond, she was gone.

I wonder who that is? he thought, looking back at her as she continued to talk and laugh on her phone.

While standing there, he heard someone else say "Jimmy Smith, how are you, my friend?"

"Gene Harper. It's been a while!" said Mr. Smith as he turned and saw his old high school buddy.

They shook hands and hugged just like in the old times.

"Man, it's really good to see you. How are you doing?" said Gene.

"I'm good, I really am."

"Call me when you can, Jimmy," said Gene as he scribbled his phone number on the back of a business card. "We have a lot of catching up to do."

"I will," he said turning the card over to see what his friend was doing these days. It read:

No Deadlines   No Obligations

Retired

Ask Someone Else

Mon -Sun   Don't Call
Not My Problem   Don't Email

Mr. Smith laughed and hugged his friend again. At that moment he knew he was going to be okay. He was back, and it was all because of his new friends . . . the CLUB US crew.

CHAPTER 2
(إثنان)
~ <u>ith</u>-nah ~

Ralph's Supermarket was bustling as always. Mr. Smith grabbed a grocery cart and unfolded his shopping list for tomorrow's big celebration. As he walked the aisles, even the grocery store seemed different. He usually parked his car in the back, got what he needed and exited as quickly as he had entered. Today he took his time choosing the best fruit, talking to people he had never met before, and enjoying the shopping experience.

Finally, he had everything he needed to make

a delicious holiday meal for his friends and their families to enjoy. At the checkout counter, he opened his folding shopping cart and loaded the bags inside. He filled the cart to the top and headed home. He had forgotten how delightful it was to take a leisure walk to the grocery store. It was something he and Elizabeth often did together, and he had blocked it from his mind. As he returned home, he greeted more neighbors along the way, and thought of his dear Elizabeth with happiness.

Once home, he unloaded the groceries and started preparations for the next day's meal. He was going to barbeque ribs, chicken, and fish and prepare Elizabeth's favorite side dishes, which included potato salad, coleslaw, baked beans, fries, and her famous carrot cake for dessert. He had even purchased fireworks and was planning a celebration after dinner, when the sun went down.

Within an hour, everything was seasoned and ready for the party. He sat down to catch a couple of game shows, and before he knew it, he had fallen asleep on the couch with the television blaring.

A knock at the door woke him. He heard the screen door opening and knew it was Eddie. That kid had more nerve than anyone he'd ever met, and he loved him for it. As far as Eddie was concerned, Mr. Smith's house was his second home, so he came over when he wanted and felt comfortable walking in just as though he lived there.

"How's it going today, Mr. Smith?" said Eddie, plopping down in his favorite chair.

"Everything's going great. I'm all set for tomorrow and looking forward to our celebration."

"Me too. This will be the first time we've all gotten together with our families, and I think it'll be fun! Do you need some help with cooking?" asked the inquisitive boy.

"I think just about everything is ready. I just have to make the carrot cake."

"Wow, I love carrot cake. Can I help you with it?"

"Sure, let's do it."

They went into the kitchen, and Eddie sat on a bar stool as Mr. Smith gathered the ingredients.

"Do you use a recipe?" asked Eddie.

"Yes, I use Elizabeth's, it's the best." He handed Eddie the laminated card with his wife's handwritten recipe.

"I think it's funny that you can make a cake with carrots."

"I thought the same thing until I tasted it, and it was delicious!" said Mr. Smith.

They both laughed and lined up the ingredients on the counter.

"So how do we cook the carrots?" asked Eddie as he grabbed the six carrots and walked over to the sink to rinse them off.

"Here you go," said Mr. Smith, handing him the grater. "Just grate them into this bowl, and I'll get the other ingredients going."

While Eddie grated the carrots, he and Mr. Smith talked and laughed, and before they knew it, the cake was in the oven. Mr. Smith made the icing, while Eddie grated some carrot curls to decorate the top. They went into the library to play a game, and within minutes they smelled the cake aroma coming out of the kitchen.

"It smells yummy." said Eddie. "Do you think we could taste it tonight?"

"No, Eddie, we're going to keep it whole until tomorrow so everyone can enjoy it together."

"Aw, Mr. Smith, that's no fun." Eddie laughed as he walked over to where B.O.R.T.R.O.N. was sitting in its glass case. Though the machine, the size of a shoebox, looked like a toy spaceship, it was the Accelerated Space and Distance (ASD) Transporter that made the CLUB US missions possible. The transporter had already taken them to Paris, Cuba, and Italy, and the entire crew was eagerly anticipating its next assignment.

"I wish B.O.R.T.R.O.N. would take us on another mission," said Eddie.

"He will, just be patient."

"I know, I know. Waiting is just so hard because the missions are a blast. Italy was so cool; I hope one day we'll be able to go back there."

"Well, you never know—maybe you will!"

Just then the timer sounded and they went into the kitchen to take the cake out of the oven. Eddie's mouth was watering, and Mr. Smith shot him a stern look from the corner of his eye. Eddie laughed because as much as he wanted to steal a piece, he didn't want his friend to be angry with him.

He really loved Mr. Smith. It was like having a grandpa he could see every day. He always made Eddie feel good when he was down in the dumps. Mr. Smith liked to play games with him, and they even cooked together. It was great. Eddie hoped his friend would always be around because he would be lost without him. Next to his dog Barks, Mr. Smith was his best friend.

CHAPTER 3
(ثلاثة)
~ tha-<u>la</u>-thah ~

"Buenas dias, Abuela," said Nikko to his grandmother as he came downstairs for breakfast. "Are you ready to go to Mr. Smith's house for the big celebration today?"

"I don't know, hijo. I've never been to an American celebration before. What will we do there?"

"We'll eat and talk, play games and laugh, just like we do at Mexican celebrations."

"Should I make some enchiladas or tamales

Evil in Egypt

to take over? I would love to do that."

"Oh, I don't know, Abuela, why don't we just eat what the Americans do. I'm sure you'll like it."

"Well, maybe I'll make a flan. Yes, that's a good idea. I'm sure they will like my flan; everyone does."

"Yes, Abuela, make a flan. They'll love it," said Nikko.

Nikko wasn't sure about taking flan to a Fourth of July celebration, but he knew his grandmother wanted to share her delicacy with the Americans so they could see what a great cook she was. Besides, his CLUB US friends liked his grandmother's flan a lot, so he thought maybe the other guests would too.

~ ~ ~

Cassie knocked on Carla's bedroom door to remind her they were going to Mr. Smith's house in an hour. She didn't answer so Cassie knocked again.

"What is it?" asked her sister, sounding as though she had just woken up.

"Remember, we're going to a Fourth of July party today at Mr. Smith's house."

"Yes, I remember. I'll be ready to go in half an hour."

"OK, see you downstairs."

Cassie wished she and Carla were close like they used to be, but Carla had her own friends now, and there didn't seem to be any room left for Cassie in her life. She loved and admired her big sister. Too bad Carla didn't enjoy spending time with her anymore. It made Cassie sad, but she knew there was nothing she could do about it. She just shrugged her shoulders and continued to hope for the best.

Cassie headed down the stairs and saw her dad in the kitchen.

"Are you looking forward to going to Mr. Smith's house today?" she asked him.

"You know what? I am. It's been a long time since I've seen Jimmy, and he was always a good friend. We know how he feels about the loss of his wife and son, because we were all devastated when your mom died. I've always respected his wishes to be left alone, but now it seems he's changed. Just the fact that he invited us over today is huge. I think we'll all have a good time."

"Me too. Mr. Smith is really cool; you'll see," Cassie said with a smile.

~ ~ ~

Mr. Khan sat in his usual chair at the kitchen table, drinking green bean coffee and reading the Beijing Times. During the week, he read the Shanghai Daily News, but on Saturdays, it was always the Beijing Times.

"Hi, Dad," said Kian as he walked into the kitchen in his white T-shirt and jeans.

"Kian," said his dad. "Why do you wear a white T-shirt every single day? Don't you have any other color shirts to wear?"

"This is my trademark, Dad," said Kian. "Everybody knows me by my white T-shirt, and when I become a famous magician on the Las Vegas strip, it'll be easy for you to recognize me on stage."

Mr. Khan looked at his son in bewilderment. *Does he really think I wouldn't be able to recognize him on a stage in Las Vegas if he had on a different color shirt?* he thought. *That boy is so strange.* He kept hoping his son would come to his senses because he hadn't been able to figure out how to tell his family in China that their grandson wasn't going to become a neurosurgeon. It was so painful, he couldn't even think about it; .

"Morning, son," said Kian's mom as she walked into the kitchen after finishing her Tai Chi exercises. Kian wanted her to go to Gio's Gym to work out like the other American moms, but she loved her Tai Chi, and he had given up trying to convince her otherwise. Kind of like his dad trying to convince him to be a neurosurgeon—it just wasn't going to happen.

"Remember, we are going to Mr. Smith's house today for Fourth of July," said Kian, smiling in anticipation.

"I can't go," said Mr. Khan. "I'm teaching a class on Skull Base Techniques this afternoon."

"Oh, Dad, please. All the other kids in CLUB US will be there with their families. Please, Dad."

"I'm sorry, Kian, but I have to work."

Kian was disappointed. He walked into the living room to talk to his parrot, Kip.

"Why does Dad have to be a neurosurgeon?" he asked. "Why can't he be a magician, or a rap singer like me? Then he could take off a day."

Mr. Khan saw his son in the living room and realized that he didn't want to let him down. He picked up his cell phone and dialed.

~ ~ ~

"C'mon kids," said Debi Collins as she passed their bedrooms on her way downstairs to make a small breakfast before going to Mr. Smith's house.

Her husband was in the kitchen, drinking coffee. "Morning, hon," said Bill Collins as his wife walked over to the refrigerator. "How are you feeling today?"

"I'm great. I made some of mom's iced tea to take over for the party; you know it's always a big hit." Debi's mom always made iced tea with six different flavored tea bags, lots of sugar, and plenty of lemons. It was delicious, and whenever she made it at home, the family drank it like water. Of course, with all the sugar, it wasn't the healthiest drink, but this was a special occasion, and Mrs. Collins wanted to contribute to the party.

"Maybe I can take over the Yahtzee and Cornhole games to play on the lawn. I always get a kick out of rolling dice the size of Christmas gifts," said her husband, with a chuckle.

"Great idea, Dad," said Eddie as he ran down the stairs. He was so excited to go to Mr. Smith's to celebrate the Fourth of July, especially because his best friends would be there.

Gold walked into the kitchen with an enormous sign she'd made that said "Happy 4th of July" with red, white, and blue pompons around the border. "What d'ya think, guys?" she asked.

"It's amazing," said Eddie. "Can it be from both of us? I don't have anything to take."

"Sure, little brother," she said, giving him a hug. He could be a pain in the neck, but she loved the kid so much. She was so lucky to have the family she did, and she hoped they all knew it.

"Ok everybody, help me clean up the kitchen, and we'll head over soon," said Debi. "I'm excited to get to this party!"

~ ~ ~

Mr. Smith was putting the final touches on

the party decorations and keying up the music. He was nervous and excited at the same time. It was the first time anyone, besides the crew, had been to his home in a very long time, and he wanted to make sure they all had a good time. He was confident they would love the food (he had followed Elizabeth's recipes to the letter), and the weather was perfect for an outdoor celebration. There wasn't any doubt they would be surprised by the fireworks—it would be the perfect ending to a perfect day.

He looked around the kitchen and the backyard. His guests would be arriving any minute and he wanted to make sure everything was in place. He walked over to the mantel in the living room and picked up a framed photo of Elizabeth and Jimmy. It was his favorite picture of his family, and he held it to his chest. He knew he was finally on his way to a new chapter in his life, and wherever he went, they would be with him.

"Hi, Mr. Smith!" he heard as the screen door opened.

CHAPTER 4
(أربعة)
~ ar-<u>ba</u>-ah ~

"Hey, Eddie," said Mr. Smith with a smile. *That kid is special,* he thought. *No matter what, seeing him makes me feel good.*

"Debi, Bill, thank you so much for coming. It's been a tough few years for me and I hope you'll understand my decision to retreat from the world. It was the only thing I knew how to do. Thanks to Eddie, Gold and the rest of the kids, I'm back. . . and I feel good!" He hugged the Collins family members, then bent down to give Barks a pat and

Evil in Egypt

a hug.

"Thank you for coming too, Barks." Barks gave him one of his sloppy kisses and they all laughed.

"Put this pitcher of iced tea in Mr. Smith's refrigerator, Gold," said Mrs. Collins. "Remember my mom's iced tea, Mr. Smith?"

"How could I forget?"

Bill and Debi stepped into the backyard to help set up the games. They admired the fun atmosphere their neighbor had created for the afternoon and looked forward to a fun day.

The bell rang, and on the other side of the screen door stood Nikko and his family.

"Hi, Mr. Smith. My whole family came with me, and we're excited to be here! My mom, Nuria, my dad, Francisco, and my brothers Antonio and Miguel." They all shook Mr. Smith's hand and Miguel said, "thanks for inviting us."

"And this is my grandma." He put his arm

around her shoulders and continued, "We call her Abuela and you can too. It means 'grandma.'" Mrs. Martinez handed him the flan with a smile, "Espero que le gusta."

"She said she hopes you'll like it."

Mr. Smith smiled, while rubbing his stomach and said, "Gracias!" He then took a few steps to the nearby kitchen to put the flan in the refrigerator.

"We're here, Mr. Smith!"

He looked around and realized the Khan family had arrived.

"Hey Kian, thanks for coming."

"This is my mom, Vida, and my dad, Stan," said Kian. He was happy his dad had found another doctor to teach the Skull Base Techniques class, and proud that he had joined him and his mom at the party. Mr. Khan was a quiet man and did little besides work and read at home. For him to be out with his family, and people he didn't know, was special.

Mr. and Mrs. Khan held their hands together in an upright position under their chins and bowed to Mr. Smith. He bowed back and winked at Kian. It was a special moment, and the boy beamed with pride.

The doorbell rang once again and Cassie and her family walked in.

"John," said Mr. Smith with a firm handshake and big smile. "It's been way too long since we've seen each other. Thank you so much for coming today. This is a new beginning for me and having you and your family back in my life means a lot."

John Warner felt the same and put his arm around Mr. Smith's shoulders as he introduced his older daughter, Carla.

"Hey, wait. Didn't I see you walking down the street yesterday?"

"Yes," said Carla with a smile. "I said hi, but I didn't think you knew who I was. I remembered you though."

"What in the world? When did you grow up to be such a beautiful young lady? I don't know which of you is the prettiest, you or Cassie, but I'm sure your dad is proud of you both!"

Cassie felt good when she heard Mr. Smith's words and hoped they would make a difference to her sister and dad, who often teased her because of her weight. Mr. Smith was wonderful, and she was happy he was in her life again.

"Thanks Mr. Smith," she whispered in his ear before joining the rest of the group.

As Mr. Smith walked into the backyard, he saw everyone filling their plates with Elizabeth's favorite holiday dishes, which brought joy to his heart. Though it was the first time the families had all been together, both kids and parents were laughing and talking like old friends. It was exactly what he had hoped for.

Everyone sat at one of the group tables and enjoyed the food and the music.

Kian hooked his cell phone to the sound system, then announced, "Ladies and gentlemen, my name is Kian Khan, and I'm going to provide you some entertainment. I'll start with one of my best magic tricks, and then the CLUB US crew and I will perform our latest hip-hop routine."

Kian's father cringed inside but kept a straight face, especially when his wife kicked him under the table. *How in the world did I get a hip-hop dancer for a son?* It was a question he asked himself repeatedly, but never got an answer.

Kian invited Mr. Smith to the table where he had set up his props. It was the magic cup trick . . . again. The kids worried that Mr. Smith would figure it out right away and spoil the trick for Kian. As he'd done time and time in the past, Kian put a ball under one of three cups, moved them around and around, then asked Mr. Smith to choose the cup hiding the ball. Mr. Smith pointed to the cup on the right, and Kian jumped with joy.

"Sorry, it's here!" he said excitedly as he lifted the left cup. "Better luck next time, Mr. Smith."

Mr. Smith walked back to his table with a gleam in his eye. He knew the ball was under the cup on the left but choosing the one on the right was the only thing to do.

Everyone was excited for Kian. Even Mr. Khan gave his wife a surprised smile and moved forward to see more.

Kian invited the rest of the crew to the front of the backyard.

"I have choreographed several hip-hop routines, and today we are going to perform our favorite for you, the one we did in Pari—, I mean, at Patricia's birthday party last week."

The crew let out a sigh of relief. No one could know about the mission to Paris, or anywhere else. They had been warned by B.O.R.T.R.O.N. and they always heeded the transporter's instructions.

The music began, and the kids performed their hip-hip routine to perfection. Everyone in the audience applauded, and Mr. Khan stood up yelling, "Bravo, bravo!"

The other people at the party looked around at him and chuckled.

Kian couldn't believe it. Was that his dad? His mother was smiling from ear to ear, and his father came over and gave him a big hug. This can't be happening, he thought. *His dad never hugged anybody*. Kian pinched himself and it hurt, so he knew what he was feeling was true. Maybe now he could follow his dream of becoming a magician and hip-hop dancer with his dad's blessing.

"Dessert is served," said Mr. Smith as he brought the carrot cake and Abuela's flan outside. A line formed quickly, and everyone grabbed some of each.

The sun had set, and the evening was coming to an end.

The men gathered to help Mr. Smith set up the fireworks, and everyone enjoyed a display as beautiful as the annual show on the riverside. Barks hid under Eddie's chair, hoping it would soon be over. There wasn't a lot he disliked as much as fireworks, and he covered his ears to muffle the sound. The colorful sparks were met with oohs and aahs, and when the final display exploded, the group stood up and cheered. Barks slid out from under the chair and turned in circles, which was his way of saying how glad he was that the fireworks were over.

The day couldn't have gone better. Friends, food, laughter, music, magic, and fireworks . . . it was perfect.

"Thanks so much, Mr. Smith," they all said. It was the most fun they'd had as neighbors, and Mr. Smith was sure this wouldn't be the last time.

CHAPTER 5
(خمسة)
~ <u>kham</u>-sah ~

The party host waved goodbye to his guests as they headed down the front steps to go home. The day was fun, but also tiring, so Mr. Smith decided to head to bed and clean up in the morning.

As he turned to walk back into the house, he heard a sound. Buzzz, hummm, buzzz. Buzzz, hummm, buzzz. There was no doubt what that meant, and he was sure the kids would be returning soon. Crew members could hear the transporter's mission signal whereever they were.

He glanced inside the open door and sure enough, B.O.R.T.R.O.N.'s lights were flashing. He turned and saw the kids running back down the street to his house.

"Mr. Smith, did we just hear the signal?" asked Eddie and Kian as they ran up the stairs.

"Yes, you did. Let's find out what's going on."

They walked into the library and slapped high fives when they saw the flashing lights. Another mission. . . finally! They had been waiting for weeks. The crew was excited but knew it was too late for them to take off. They all told their parents they left something at Mr. Smith's house, and were expected to come home right away.

"B.O.R.T.R.O.N., we can't go on a mission right now," said Kian. "My mom and dad will be looking all over for me. Even being away for half an hour would be too much at this time of night."

"Kian's right," said Nikko, and the other kids

nodded their heads in agreement.

"Hold on, guys," said B.O.R.T.R.O.N. "I know it's too late to travel now, but I wanted to give you the information tonight so we can take off right away in the morning. Sit down and let me explain what you'll need to do. It will only take about five minutes."

The crew members were excited. Though still worried what their parents might be thinking, they sat down to learn what the mission would be. Mr. Smith joined them.

"This mission is taking us to Africa."

"Africa, oh my gosh, that's where—" began Eddie.

"Eddie, you need to stay quiet and listen," said B.O.R.T.R.O.N. "Tomorrow morning, we will travel to Egypt, the third largest country on the continent. There are over one hundred million people there, and your help is needed.

"As you may know, there are thousands of

pyramids and tombs in Egypt, some nearly five thousand years old. At one time, they were full of valuable treasures because the kings and queens believed the items would follow them into the afterlife. Unfortunately, most of the tombs have been robbed and the valuables sold around the world. One of the most famous pyramids was that of King Tutankhamun, or King Tut, as you've probably heard him called. There were over five thousand amazing objects in his tomb when Howard Carter discovered it in 1922 in the Valley of the Kings. Since then, the exhibit has traveled all over the world and many people have seen the magnificent artifacts that were allowed to leave the country on display.

"Egypt has recently completed a museum at a cost of one billion dollars . . . "

Everyone gasped!

" . . . and tomorrow they are transporting treasures there from all over the country. Trillions of dollars of valuables being brought to the new central location, and they have hired almost all the security guards in the country to protect them. All eyes will be on the procession of treasures that will make the trek from their current homes to the Grand Egyptian Museum in Cairo."

"That's amazing," said Cassie, "but what do we need to do?"

"In Saqqara, where the oldest tombs in all of Egypt are found, archaeologists, historians, and Egyptologists recently discovered the tomb of King Wahtee. When they entered, they found walls filled with hieroglyphics that told the story of the king and queen, and their family. After carefully surveying and recording everything in the first passageway, they noticed a section of the floor that appeared to have a door. The wiped the sand away from the door and opened it. Moving the light to the opening, they saw a narrow shaft with a ladder leaning against it. They descended, carrying the light with them. At the bottom was a hallway with three chambers, each guarded by gilded statues. When they opened the heavy doors of the first chamber, they saw ornate jewelry boxes filling the room. They lifted the lids carefully, and piles and piles of turquoise, azul, amethyst, gold, silver, copper, and more were revealed. The sight nearly blinded the archaeologists, and they knew they had unearthed something that would change history. There were so many jewels that the sparkles reflected off the walls full of ancient art and created colorful light that was almost blinding.

"They reported their find to the Egyptian government and started to categorize the jewels for eventual inclusion in the new museum."

"It's getting late, B.O.R.T.R.O.N. I'm afraid you're going to have to explain the rest of the mission in the morning. What time do they need to be here to take off?"

"You're right, James. Meet me tomorrow at

8:00 a.m. so we can get going as soon as possible," said B.O.R.T.R.O.N. "I will give you the rest of the details after we take off."

"And here are some pieces of cake to take home to explain why you came back tonight," said Mr. Smith. He had thought of everything, and the kids smiled in appreciation.

The crew members grabbed their pieces of cake and ran out of the door. They couldn't have moved faster because as soon as they got to the front steps, they saw Gold and Eddie's dad coming back to Mr. Smith's house to look for them.

"Hey, what are you guys up to?" he asked calmly. *Dad is so cool,* thought Gold and Eddie.

"We just came back to pick up some cake to bring home," said Eddie.

"Well, come on," he said as the other kids crossed the street to go home. "Let's walk Nikko to his house. It's kind of late for him to go alone."

CHAPTER 6
(ستّة)
~ <u>seh</u>-tah ~

Sleep was hard to come by for the CLUB US crew. They'd gone on enough missions to know that adventure, fun, and danger lay ahead of them the next morning. Traveling with B.O.R.T.R.O.N. was the most exciting thing they had ever done, and so far, so good. They had completed all their missions and returned home safely, and were ready to go again.

No matter what, however, there was always the fear that if they weren't successful, thousands, maybe even millions, of lives could be lost.

Nikko lay in bed and thought about their first mission to Paris when he had to dismantle the explosive device inside the Eiffel Tower restaurant. He had tried the first time and failed. He'd attempted it a second time with no luck. Wiping sweat from his brow, he'd tried a third time, and. . . he couldn't think about it anymore. It was so frightening.

Cassie remembered what happened when they had to dive into the ocean near Cuba and stop an oil drilling rig that had caused a ridge on the surface of the earth under the ocean. The kids knew that if the drilling continued, it could ignite the largest volcano in the world. If the volcano erupted, the entire island and much of the Caribbean, including the wide variety of marine animals, would have been destroyed. Cassie had been certified to dive deeper than the others, so the responsibility was with her, and a professional diver, to make it happen. They dove but couldn't find the switch to stop the drilling. Suddenly, they noticed a shark swimming directly toward them.

The first thing that both Eddie and Gold thought of as they tried to fall asleep was their mission to Italy. The crew had been tasked with halting the computers belonging to Berti Motors. All the computers had been programmed to simultaneously melt down millions of Galotta vehicles, including cars, trucks, buses, ambulances, train cars, and more, throughout the country. It was especially scary for Eddie and Gold because they were born in Italy and had a special connection to the country. The team was running out of time and had to leave the data center to return to B.O.R.T.R.O.N. before the technicians had stopped the computers. Now, the kids had to trust that the techs would make it happen. . . but how could they be sure?

And Kian thought about Egypt. He had no

idea how they were going to pull it off, but he was confident that B.O.R.T.R.O.N. had a plan.

Finally, five pairs of eyes closed, and the kids were able to get some sleep before they took off on their fourth mission.

CHAPTER 7
(سبعة)
~ <u>saa</u>-bah ~

The CLUB US crew met up at Mr. Smith's house bright and early the next morning. Their parents had become used to the idea of them hanging out with their neighbor when they weren't in school, so their early departure didn't raise any eyebrows at home.

To their surprise, when they entered the library, B.O.R.T.R.O.N.'s door was standing open. The crew expected a quick departure, but the open door told them they would be boarding immediately. They quickly formed a circle and touched fingertips in the middle. Even though this was their fourth trip, they never got used to shrinking down to two inches in height to travel. Mr. Smith picked them up, one by one, and set them on the desk.

As always, Eddie didn't want to leave Barks. He walked to the edge of the desk and Barks stood on his back paws to give him one of his goodbye kisses. Eddie saw the wet tongue coming toward him and knew he would be totally drenched at his miniature height, so he ran in the transporter's door, waving goodbye to his canine friend.

"Bye, Barks! I'll be back soon."

Barks was used to it by now and looked forward to spending the time with Mr. Smith. He gave Eddie a goodbye bark and turned around to head for the living room. He liked lying on the floor near the couch while Mr. Smith watched his game shows. Barks's favorite was Name That

Tune because there was a lot of music playing, and it helped him fall into his afternoon dog-siesta.

After the crew members boarded the transporter, they sat down and their seat belts automatically buckled around them.

B.O.R.T.R.O.N. began. "A team of defense specialists from the country of Qumar is planning an attack on their neighbor, Borduria. The two countries have been fighting for centuries, both trying to control land in the Simbal region that they each contend belongs to them. Qumar has built a missile and plans to destroy an enormous area of Borduria with it. The device, however, needs a metal that has only been found in ancient Egypt. If the specialists can obtain a quantity of the naturally occurring alloy, elureum, and add it to the explosive, it will result in ten times the amount of destruction that would occur without it.

"Elureum only existed in the Fifth Dynasty in ancient Egypt. Once the empire crumbled, the metal disappeared and has not been found elsewhere in the world.

"The Qumarian defense team became aware of the discovery of the tomb of King Wahtee and his wife, Garensi. The team also learned that these leaders had an obsession with jewels and precious metals. Like most royals of the Fifth Dynasty, Wahtee and Garensi had amassed a wealth of elureum and had it buried in their tomb, along with the other treasures they believed they would need in the next life.

"To achieve their plan, the Qumarians contacted Mohammed Yusef, the head of the archaeological team working on the tomb's excavation. They couldn't tell him the truth, so they told him they needed the metal to make into a powder to be combined with medical ingredients that would help thousands of their people suffering from fatal diseases.

"Mohammed refused to help them. He

explained that he could not grant their request because it was illegal to allow finds from Egyptian tombs to leave the country, and that he would be severely punished if he allowed it to happen. They came back again and again and implored him to accept their offer. They explained each time that because so many people in their country were dying from incurable diseases, thousands of lives would be saved with his aid. Every time, he refused.

"Finally, the Qumarians offered Mohammed a sum of money far larger than what he could ever amass in a lifetime. He still said no but continued to think about the help he could offer his mother, who was recently diagnosed with cancer. He knew that taking a small amount of the ancient metal from the enormous quantity of jewels and other artifacts found in the tomb would probably go unnoticed. He would never do anything that would bring shame to his country, but he needed to help his mother. No one was more important to him than her, and his family could not afford the medical treatments she would need.

"Mohammed still wasn't sure if it was the right thing to do, but finally, he contacted the Qumarians. He told them he would do what they asked and explained that it would take several weeks, if not months, as he could only take a small amount at a time.

"He cautioned the Qumarians that he didn't know if his team members would find elureum, but if they did, he would take the quantity they were requesting. Months passed until one day, when his team was inventorying the gold, silver, copper, and other precious metals, he heard someone asking about a metal he had never seen before.

"'That is elureum,' another team member responded. 'I can tell by the pale color. In ancient Egypt, elureum was as valuable as gold or silver, but it had a particular property that allowed it to be used for other purposes as well. I've heard of it being ground and used in medicine, mummification materials, and skin care products that the queens used to protect their skin from the sun.'

"Mohammed learned where the elureum was being stored, and when he had a chance, he examined the metal. It was very lightweight and had a distinctive color.

"The Qumarians gave him a deadline. They knew that almost all the security guards in Egypt would be protecting the treasures that were being transported to the Grand Egyptian Museum three months later, and they wanted to take advantage of the moment to get the elureum out of the country. Mohammed agreed and told them he would begin moving small quantities of the metal to a secret hiding place inside the tomb.

"Each week, he sent them a signal to let them know things were progressing as planned. And even though he was still torn about the decision he made, Mohammed wanted to help his mother, and thought this was the only way."

"It sounds like Mohammed Yusef is a good man," said Nikko.

"He is, and you must find him and tell him the truth. Once he learns that the lives of the Bordurians, who have as much right to the land as the Qumarians, will be in danger, he will not give the elureum to their defense team.

"You will arrive in Cairo, at the site of the Pyramids of Giza, the largest in the world. Mohammed's brother, Abdul, is the owner of a camel-riding stable there. Explain the situation to him. If he doesn't believe you, show him this picture. It is a picture of him, Mohammed, and their brother, Amman, as children at home with their parents."

The kids heard the photo shoot out from the slot in the computer, and Gold grabbed it. She passed it around for everyone to see.

"He will at least listen to what you have to

say because he'll know you would not have this photo unless you had a connection to his family," said B.O.R.T.R.O.N.

"Once you meet Mohammed, show him this," continued B.O.R.T.R.O.N. as another piece of paper shot out of the computer. "It is a diagram of the inside of the tomb, with an X over the spot where he has hidden the elureum. He will believe you when he sees it.

"Are you ready?" asked B.O.R.T.R.O.N.

"We're ready," said Cassie.

Everyone looked at her in disbelief. Cassie always disbelieved everything. Was it possible that she was now agreeing to the mission without needing more convincing?

"Yes, you heard me right," she said. "We're ready!"

They all smiled, and Gold gave her a big hug. Something had happened to change her attitude, and the rest of the crew wasn't going to question it. They were just happy that she was on board right away because she always came through for the team.

"Grab your Egyptian pounds, translators, food, and high-speed cell phone chargers in case of emergency," said B.O.R.T.R.O.N.

"Wow! This is a lot of money," said Eddie.

"It looks like a lot, but keep in mind one US dollar is worth 15.60 Egyptian pounds," said B.O.R.T.R.O.N.

"So, if we buy a Coca-Cola, we're probably looking at almost 50 pounds! That's crazy!" said Kian.

They all laughed and grabbed their necessities.

They felt themselves land and, looking out the window, saw they were high up.

"You're on one of the steps of the Great Pyramid. I landed in the back, where tourists usually don't go, so you'll have time to grow back to size, then get to the bottom and find Abdul.

"I'll be here tomorrow morning at 8:27. Good luck, and don't be late!"

They exited the transporter, the door closed, B.O.R.T.R.O.N. took off, and they felt themselves resuming their normal sizes.

It was showtime!

CHAPTER 8
(ثمانية)
~ <u>tha</u>-maa-nee-ah ~

As the kids ran down the steps on the backside of the Great Pyramid, they joined the tourists in front who were admiring the breathtaking ancient architecture. The kids were in awe and couldn't believe that it had been built more than 4,500 years ago.

"I wonder how they got the slabs to the top," said Cassie. "In those days, they didn't have the machinery we do today, did they?"

"No, they didn't," said Nikko. "The Great

CLUB US

Pyramid of Giza took twenty thousand workers twenty years to do it. No one really knows how they managed it because it was impossible for human beings to lift the enormous stone blocks. Each one weighs thousands of pounds. Some people think they used sleds or water to slide the blocks to the top. I doubt if we'll ever really know their method, but it obviously was successful."

As always, the CLUB US crew was amazed that Nikko knew so much. Eddie gave him a high five, and Nikko heard his other friends shouting, "Epic! Awesome! Cool!"

Gold smiled at him; she was always learning something from Nikko and couldn't imagine what the group would do without him. She hoped his parents never moved back to Mexico!

"Hey guys, I see some camels," said Kian, beckoning for them to follow him. As they walked, they saw more and more camel stables and began feeling doubtful that they could find Abdul.

Evil in Egypt

Eddie repeated into his translator, "Do you know where Abdul is?" and heard "Hal taelam ayin Abdul?" (هل تعلم اين عبدول؟) . He knew Arabic was spoken in Egypt and hoped he could handle the translation. He walked up to the first stable and repeated, "Hal taelam ayin eabdul?" Everyone laughed, but no one seemed to know him.

"Camel ride, my friend?" said a man at a nearby stable. Eddie repeated the phrase to the man, who said, "Nice accent, my friend, but I don't know him."

"How are we going to find this guy?" said Kian. "There are so many camel stables."

"Why don't we split up and see if we have better luck?" said Gold.

"Good idea, Gold," said Nikko.

They split up and walked around the area, looking for Abdul. Finally, Cassie got lucky.

"Hey, guys," she shouted and waved them over. They all walked over to where Cassie was talking to one of the stable owners.

" . . . and he didn't come in today to work," said the young man.

Cassie turned to the crew and explained, "This is Abdul's little brother, Amman. Abdul runs the stable, but he's not here today. Amman is working in his place."

"Can you help us find him?" asked Gold.

"Who are you?" asked Amman with distrust.

"We are members of CLUB US, and we're here to help your brother Mohammed. We were told that Abdul could get us to him."

Amman looked surprised. How do these kids know so much about my big brothers? he wondered.

"Laa, laa," (لا) said Amman, shaking his head. He turned away from them because he didn't know why they wanted to see his brothers, and he wasn't going to give them any information.

"Look," said Gold. "This should prove to

you that we're telling the truth."

Amman looked at the picture of his family, which included him sitting in a highchair as a baby. He jumped back with surprise and stared at the kids with wary eyes.

"How do you have this picture of my family?" asked Amman.

"Please, just take us to Mohammed, and we'll explain everything," said Gold.

Amman pulled out his cell phone and made a call. He spoke in Arabic for a few minutes, then turned to the kids and said, "OK, I will take you to him. I will close the stable in one hour, and then we will go to my home for lunch."

"Great," said Gold.

"Can we take a ride on your camels before we leave? We can pay you," said Eddie.

"Yes, that's a good idea. You can get some practice because we will have to ride the camels home."

"Cool!" said Kian.

The camels were kneeling on the ground. Kian and Eddie hopped on the back of one of them. Gold took a camel all to herself, and Nikko and Cassie rode one together.

Amman said, "Hayaa bina" (هيا بنا قم) to the camels. They quickly stood and started walking to the right of the pyramid.

"Where are we going?" asked Cassie.

"The camels know the route by heart. They walk it every day, and you are very safe. They will take you on a tour of the pyramids and the Sphinx, and bring you back here in half an hour," said Amman.

"Oh my gosh," said Cassie as she squirmed to find a comfortable spot on the back of the huge animal. "I don't know about this."

This is the doubting Cassie we know, her friends thought as they relaxed into the backs of the camels to start their tour.

Evil in Egypt

The animals walked slowly but seemed to know where they were going. Now that the kids were settled on the backs of the tall animals, they saw everything from a different perspective. The tourists seemed to disappear below them, and they looked out into a desert with fine beige sand that swirled and lifted as if making a statement about its grandeur. From their vantage point, the half-man, half-animal Sphinx looked even more majestic than when they were on the ground. The pyramids came alive with golden sunrays that cast shadows and light on every side. They saw a unique and symmetrical view of the nine pyramids lined up one after the other and felt like they were on a movie lot in Hollywood.

It was also funny to see traffic, buildings, cafés, a golf course, and homes just outside the ancient structures. Cairo was a mix of old and new and everything Egyptian mixed into one.

Finally, the camels headed back to Amman's

stable. When they arrived, he was packing up to go home. He handed each of the kids a pair of white pants and a white shirt, along with a white band.

"Wear these clothes on top of your own and tie the band around your head. We have to walk through the middle of town, and we don't want people to wonder who you are," said Amman, handing each of them an outfit to wear.

"Me gusta!" said Nikko. He only expressed his like for something in Spanish when he was really excited about it, so everyone knew this was special for him.

"Arak lahiqan," (أراك لاحقا), Amman said to his buddies, waving goodbye and jumping on the camel with Gold.

"What does that mean?" asked Gold.

"It means 'see you later' in our language," said Amman. "ah-rahk lah-hair-kun ," he repeated, happy that the kids were interested in his language.

These American kids are cool, thought

Amman. He was taking them to his home, so he hoped they were telling the truth. If they weren't, he was going to be in big trouble with his brothers . . . both of them.

"OK, follow me," said Amman. "The camels know the way home, but there will be a lot of traffic, so we have to be careful."

"Traffic?" said Cassie. "Do you mean the camels will walk in the middle of the street?"

"Yes," said Amman with a laugh. "That's how it works."

"Crazy," said Cassie, hanging on tightly to Nikko.

CHAPTER 9
(تاسعة)
~ taa-say-<u>ah</u> ~

Amman led the camels in and out of traffic, just like he was driving a car, and the CLUB US crew followed behind with no problem. The camels even knew to stop at a red light and to take off when it turned green. No one paid them any attention; it was obvious that camels walking alongside morning traffic was nothing unusual.

As they navigated the boulevard, the kids noticed the office buildings and apartments, cafés, stores and boutiques, and crowds of people.

"This reminds me of Paris," said Gold.

"Yeah, it does," said Kian, "but way more people and I don't remember seeing any camels walking down the street there," he continued with a laugh.

"OK, we're going to turn left at the next corner," said Amman, turning around and speaking to the others over the sounds of the cars.

The three camels took a left at the next corner and, about halfway down the block, turned into an entranceway with a gate.

"This is my home," Amman said, jumping down from the camel and indicating to the others to do the same. He opened the gate, and the camels walked over to where their lunch was waiting.

"Wow, they're well trained, aren't they?" said Nikko.

"Well, not all the time," said Amman with a laugh, as he walked up the stairs.

Before they got to the top, they heard the

camels' bleating.

"What's going on?" said Amman, turning and running down the stairs. "Oh no! We didn't lock the gate behind us, and now they're running away," he said with a frightened look on his face. "Come on, you must help me catch them; my brothers will kill me if they are lost or stolen. They are the only way our family can make enough money to eat."

They all hurried out of the gate and saw the camels racing down the street.

"Kef! Kef!" (قف, قف!) yelled Amman as he raced after them.

The kids followed, also yelling, "Kef! Kef!"

Friends and neighbors ran with them. It was obvious what had happened, and they wanted to help catch the Yusef family's animals.

Everyone was yelling, "Kef! Kef!", but the more they yelled, the faster the camels ran.

They raced past tourists who were afraid,

and bystanders who found the spectacle amusing. Drivers jumped out of their cars, screaming at the camels and at the kids behind them. It was a chaotic scene and even though they were getting closer, Amman and the kids couldn't quite catch them.

At that moment, a huge truck turned the corner, completely blocking the street. The camels had no choice but to stop, and the kids caught up. Amman and his neighbors grabbed the ropes around the camels' necks to stop them from running away again.

Once the camels were under control, Amman walked over and said in a loud voice, "Madha tafael!? ماذا تفعل!؟"

Cassie repeated it into her translator. The crew heard the machine say, "What are you doing?" and they all laughed.

The camels were like little kids who had gotten into trouble. Amman told them to kneel, and they did, right in the middle of all the traffic and chaos. He walked around to each of them and stared at them with cold eyes. They bowed their heads like humans would do, and it looked as though they wanted to say, "I'm sorry." They were adorable. The Americans felt sorry for them and hoped Amman would be nice.

"C'mon guys," said Amman to his new friends. "Get on and they will take us home."

They all mounted the camels and turned to head back to Amman's house. When they arrived, his mom was standing outside with her arms folded. The kids recognized her look and knew they were in trouble. Apparently, moms all over the world were the same. When they were angry, there were going to be consequences.

I hope I won't have to wash pots and pans in Egypt, thought Eddie as they put the camels back into the yard.

Amman carefully locked the gate and double-checked it before mounting the stairs behind his mom. The CLUB US crew followed.

Once inside the house, Amman and his mom started talking, and the Americans knew exactly what was going on. Even though the language was different, they could tell Amman was trying to talk his way out of a punishment.

Then he had an idea. He grabbed his mom's hand and led her over to where the kids were standing. "Mom, these are my new friends," Amman said in English. "They're here to talk to Mohammed. Look at the photo they have of our family," he continued, pulling the photo from his pocket.

His mom looked at the photo, then she looked at the kids, then she looked at the photo again. She walked closer to them and gazed into each of their eyes with a stern look. Amman was nervous, as he didn't know what she was going to do or say.

Finally, a big smile appeared on her face, and

she said in a warm voice, "Marhaban!" (مرحبا!)

They didn't know what it meant, but they knew it was good, so they responded, "Marhaban!" Amman's mom gave them each a big hug and pointed to a table full of delicious-looking food she had prepared for lunch. Amman moved extra chairs to the table, and they all sat down. His mom went into the kitchen and brought out more plates filled with amazing food.

"This is what we eat in Egypt at lunch, and even sometimes at dinner. I hope you like it. My favorite is Kushari," Amman said as he pointed to a dish that looked like art. "It's a mix of rice, spaghetti, macaroni, vermicelli, fried onions, black lentils, and hummus. On top is a sauce made with tomatoes, garlic and vinegar sauce, and chili peppers. It's great!"

"This one is also delicious. It's called Mulukhiya and is a chopped green vegetable like spinach cooked with meat and garlic. Here's some rice to eat with it. Everybody in Egypt eats Mulukhiya, and it's prepared differently in different parts of the country. Sometimes it's made with beef or chicken, and people who live near the coast make it with fish or shrimp. My mom cooks it with . . . hmmm . . . how do I say arnab (أرنب) in English?"

"Rabbit," he heard a voice say. Everyone turned and saw two men entering the room.

"Right, rabbit!" said Amman. "These are my brothers, Mohammed and Abdul."

The kids all smiled and waved, and the brothers walked over to the table with puzzled looks on their faces.

"These are my new friends from California that I called and told you about. Guys, introduce yourselves to my brothers."

"Hi, I'm Gold. This is Eddie, Nikko, Cassie, and Kian," she said, pointing to each of the crew members. "Nice to meet you."

"Nice to meet you too," said Abdul, "but why are you here?"

"Let's eat and they'll explain later," said Amman. He didn't want his brother to know that he was also clueless as to why the kids were there. He believed they had an important reason for wanting to talk to his big brother, and he wanted the family to give them a chance.

Mrs. Yusef came in from the kitchen with more food and gave her other two sons a kiss on both cheeks before sitting down.

"Abi Hal toried an ta'akul?" (هل تريد أن تأكل؟) she said to the old man in the corner.

"Leh (ال)," he responded.

"That's my grandpa, and he doesn't eat much. He likes to sits near the window and look out or practice backgammon," said Amman.

"I like backgammon," said Nikko. "Maybe I can play a game with him later."

"That would be funny," said Amman. "I'd

like to see you beat him," he continued with a laugh.

There was so much amazing-looking food, the kids didn't know what to try first.

"You know felafel and kebobs, right? And there's also fatta and ful medames. It's all great, so dig in!" Amman said.

Everyone at the table scooped some of each dish onto his or her plate and started to eat. The room became quiet as they all enjoyed the variety of dishes. The kids were surprised how good everything was. Before today they didn't know what people in Egypt ate, but now that they did, they wanted more.

When they were almost done, Amman's mom returned to the dining room with four plates of dessert. She put them on the table, one at a time, and Amman announced, "Kunafa Zalabiya, Om Ali, and my favorite Kahk cookies. Trust me; they're amazing, and you're going to love them all!"

He was right. The desserts were some of the best the crew members had ever eat-en. They recognized the taste of dates, nuts, raisins, coconut flakes, honey, and white and dark chocolate, just like at home.

"How do you say thank you, Amman?" asked Eddie to break the ice.

"Shukran!" answered Amman.

"Shukran, shukran, shukran," repeated the kids. "This food is wonderful!"

Finally, there was tea for everyone, and then the table was silent again. Amman's mom went into the kitchen to wash the dishes, and the Yusef brothers stared at the kids.

Nikko said, "We are here for a very important reason, and it's something we need to discuss with Mohammed."

"Anything you have to say to me, you can say in front of my family. We don't have secrets," said Mohammed with a serious face.

Hesitantly, Nikko pulled out the diagram of the chamber in the Wahtee tomb and placed it in front of Mohammed. The elder Yusef brother's face turned pale.

"Where did you get this?"

"We have been sent here to help you, Mohammed. We know of the plan you have with the Qumarian officials, and we understand why you did it, but the information we have will give you a different perspective that we think will make you change your mind."

"What are they talking about, Mohammed?" asked Abdul.

Mohammed closed his eyes and covered his face with his hands.

Amman didn't say a word, as he and his brother Abdul knew not to push him to answer. Ever since their father died, Mohammed had become the head of their family. They always listened to him, and he always made the best decisions for them.

"You have made a mistake," Mohammed finally said. "I have no idea what you are talking about, and it's now time for you to leave."

He stood up, and the expression on his strong face was frightening to them all, including his brothers.

The kids didn't know what to say or do. It was clear he knew what was going on but denied it. Now, they would have to find another way to stop the elureum from getting into the hands of the Qumarians.

The kids stood up and again thanked the brothers for the food and hospitality. Amman looked sad because he liked the kids and wanted to help them, but he knew he could never cross his brother. It's just not how things were done in their country.

The kids walked past the kitchen and said

shukran to Mrs. Yusef. She gave them a big smile and hug and touched each of their faces with her small, warm hands. Cassie had checked her translator and said, "ma alsalama" (ما السلامة) to her, which meant "goodbye."

The tension in the room was unbearable. The kids knew the faster they left, the better. They walked out the door and down the stairs. Amman followed.

"I am very sorry," he said. "But my brother is the head of our household, and we can never go against anything he says."

"We understand, and we appreciate everything you've done for us. Shukran," said Gold.

CHAPTER 10
(عاشرة)
~ <u>ah</u>-shee-rah ~

"Are we really standing in the middle of the street in Cairo, Egypt, with no idea of what to do next, or am I dreaming?" said Cassie.

"You're not dreaming; we are living a nightmare right now," said Gold as they turned left from Amman's house. "I wish we could wake up."

"He didn't even give us a chance," said Kian. "That's not fair."

"Who told you life is fair?" said Cassie. "It's not, my friend."

Evil in Egypt

Gold wished Cassie would stop thinking so negatively. Now wasn't the time to bring the mood down even further than it was.

They had to come up with a Plan B, and they had to do it quickly. They walked to the corner, not quite sure what to do. They quietly strolled down the boulevard, each searching his or her brain for an alternate plan.

Cairo was modern and cosmopolitan. Gold was right; almost everything about the city reminded them of Paris, except, of course, for the camels that weaved in and out of traffic. They demanded as much right to the street as the hundreds of vehicles, whose owners were honking their horns and playing loud music. There were huge build-ings everywhere, along with tall palm trees and shops of all sorts. Tourists spoke Eng-lish and other languages right alongside Egyptians who made Arabic sound melodic and exotic. Cairo was more than five thousand years old, but today the old and the new mixed together perfectly. There was rap music playing in one restaurant and traditional Egyptian tunes drifted out of the windows next door. Many women wore jeans and T-shirts, others sported modern clothing with scarves covering their heads, and some dressed in the traditional abayas and hijabs that only revealed their eyes. Men were equally diverse: jeans, business suits, and casual clothes mixed with gallibiyas, V-neck caftans that stretched to the ground. Every tradition came together with mutual respect, and it was nice to see.

They arrived at a café at the corner. It was full of men playing chess and women smoking hookahs. There were tiny cups of expresso coffee at many of the tables, and waiters ran back and forth to serve people from all walks of life. The scene looked like something out of Indiana Jones, but instead of excitement, the CLUB US crew was feeling hopeless.

They saw another café with yellow tables and chairs on the other side of the street and crossed the congested street, careful not to get run over by a car or a camel.

After taking a seat at a table near the sidewalk, they ordered fresh fruit smoothies and observed the Pyramids of Giza. The structures were spectacular and reminded the kids that they had a very important mission to complete, and not much time to do it.

The waiter took their order, and the club members leaned forward to talk.

"Since we couldn't convince Mohammed to listen to us, we have no other option than to go to the tomb and steal the elureum ourselves," said Gold. "If Mohammed gives it to the Qumarians, many lives will be lost, and he will be responsible."

Their smoothies arrived and after paying their bill, they heard the synchronized footsteps of armed guards walking by. They were installing police barriers around the city in preparation for the next day's transmission of the artifacts. The kids had never seen so many military guards, and it reinforced to them just how important tomorrow's procession would be. They also understood why the Qumarians chose this day to pull off the theft of the elureum from the tomb in Saqqara.

"Ahlan, (أهلا)" they heard a voice say from behind Cassie's chair.

"Mohammed!" said Eddie, excitedly.

Mohammed pulled up a chair and joined the kids. He put his elbows on the table and thought about what he wanted to say.

The tension was tight at the table. The kids knew Mohammed had something important to tell them, or he wouldn't have sought them out. Everyone stayed quiet and waited for him to speak first.

"I am sorry for my behavior at the house," he began. "When I saw the drawing, I knew you were aware of my involvement with the Qumarians and it wasn't something I could discuss in front of my family. Since my father died, my mother and brothers look to me for guidance and to set a good example for each of them.

"I don't make very much money as an archaeologist, and though many people admire the work I do, it's more of an honorable obligation to my country than a way to provide for my mother and brothers. That's why we have the camel stable at the pyramid. Without it, we wouldn't be able to survive.

"When the Qumarians offered me money to give them some of the elureum in the tomb we were excavating, I rejected their offer. How could I dishonor my country and possibly my father's name by doing such a thing? They continued to contact me and explained that the precious metal would be used in medicine to save lives in Qumar, and I knew this was also an honorable endeavor for me to support. For months I refused to cooperate, but finally, when I learned my mother had cancer and would need expensive treatment, I decided to comply. I knew it was illegal, but I also knew my actions might save my mother's life, along with thousands of Qumarians who were in need of medication.

"Why are you here? Are you working with the Qumarians? I've already agreed to do what they want, so I don't understand who you are or what you want from me."

The kids felt bad for Mohammed. He thought he was doing the right thing and they would have to explain to him that the Qumarians had duped him.

Gold began. "Mohammed, I am very sorry to tell you this, but the Qumarians did not tell you the truth."

Mohammed straightened in his chair, a puzzled look on his face.

"What do you mean?" he said.

"The Qumarians are planning to launch a missile on Borduria, and if they add elureum to the explosive, it will make the force of the missile ten times stronger and destroy many more lives. You must not let it happen, Mohammed. We know you wouldn't want to bear the responsibility for the devastation that would occur if you complied with them."

Gold wanted to say more, but when she saw a tear falling from Mohammed's eye, she knew he had heard enough.

Mohammed started to pray in Arabic, and the kids remained silent.

After several minutes, he raised his head and said, "Thank you so much for bringing me the truth. I hope Allah will forgive me."

"He will Mohammed; you are a good man," said Eddie as he gave him a hug.

Mohammed smiled and said, "Your diagram

shows that you know where my hiding place is. I planned to go there tonight to get the elureum and give it to the Qumarians at midnight. What should I do now?"

"When you speak to them, explain that you know the truth, and that you cannot give them the metal," said Nikko.

"I can't do that. They have men stationed around my home. If I don't do what they say, I'm afraid they will harm my family and my neighbors. I can't let that happen."

"Is there any other way we could keep them from getting it?" Cassie asked.

"I don't know," said Mohammed. "I really don't know, but maybe . . ."

"Why don't you make an anonymous call to the police to warn them and leave the elureum in a spot they can stake out to arrest the Qumarians when they come to pick it up," said Eddie.

"That's a great idea," said Kian.

"I don't know," said Mohammed. "Do you really think it could work? They are expecting me to bring it directly to them."

"Just tell them people are watching you and that it will be safer for everyone if you just leave it for them to pick up," said Nikko.

"I guess that could work," said Mohammed. "I guess."

He was afraid of the Qumarians, but he kept his father's face in front of his eyes and knew he had to do what he would have expected of him.

"Yes, I will do it," he said. "I will go to the tomb in Saqqara, get the elureum, and leave it near the Step Pyramid. It is the oldest pyramid in Egypt, built 2600 BC, and no one pays it much attention anymore because all the treasures have already been removed," said Mohammed.

"That will work," said Gold. "Here's my cell number. Will you call me once everything has been taken care of so we can return home, knowing no harm will be done to the people of Qumar?"

"Yes, I will. It is three o'clock. I will go there now and call you once the police have arrested the Qumarians."

"Shukran, Mohammed," said Gold.

All the kids gave Mohammed a hug, and he left the café, heading to Saqqara.

CHAPTER 11
(إحادي عشر)
~ <u>eh</u>-dah ah-<u>shar</u> ~

The kids relaxed.

"Was it really that easy?" asked Eddie.

"I think so," said Gold, with a slight hesitation.

"When something sounds too good to be true, it usually is. I'm just saying," said Cassie.

"I think we're good," said Gold.

"Me too. We're CLUB US, and we're getting better and better at this with each mission," said Kian.

They all laughed and decided to go for a walk.

Cairo was a huge city with a population of over twenty million. They saw people of all ages, and the city jumped with activity.

Soon they arrived at a street full of stalls with people selling everything from house shoes to furniture. Every vendor tried to convince tourists who walked by their shops to buy something from them.

"I have good deal for you, my friend, only one dollar," said one of the men.

"One dollar?" asked Eddie.

"Yes, my friend, take a look."

"No, Eddie," said Gold. "We have no way to carry items around; we're here for one reason, and it's not to go shopping."

"Sorry," said Eddie to the man.

They continued down the street and saw merchants in business deals, people haggling over

Evil in Egypt

prices, and lots of cats everywhere.

"I've never seen so many cats in my life," said Cassie. She had a couple at home herself, but in Cairo they were everywhere. They walked in and out of all the stalls, hid under tables in the cafés, and even climbed on benches in parks next to people. It was clear that Egypt liked cats, and cats also liked Egypt.

"Yikes, I'm so scared of cats," said Gold.

"You are? Why? They won't bother you," said Cassie.

"I know, but I've been afraid of them all my life, and seeing them all over the place here is giving me the heebie-jeebies."

"She's telling the truth," said Eddie. "She's even afraid to look at cat food commercials on TV. Gold, remember that time a cat came into the house with the mailman, and you were so scared you lost your voice? Mom had to take you to the hospital."

"Of course I remember," said Gold. "It was a nightmare."

"We didn't know that," said Cassie.

"Yeah, I try not to show it because I know it doesn't make sense, but when you're afraid, you're afraid."

Finally, they reached the end of the market and no one had bought anything, except a dog toy Eddie had managed to secretly purchase for Barks. He put it in his pocket and planned to keep it there until he got home.

"Look at that sign. It says ZOO!" shouted Kian.

"Awesome, let's go there," said Cassie.

They continued down the street and saw an ice cream stand. Cairo was a lot hotter than at home in Hamilton City, and they each bought a two-scoop cone to cool down.

They sat in a crowded park across the street to enjoy their treats. They were so grateful that

Mohammed believed them and had agreed to spoil the Qumarians' plans.

"I hope he'll call soon to tell us he has hidden the elureum behind the Step Pyramid and called the police to arrest the Qumarians when they pick it up," said Gold.

"I hope so too," said Cassie. "I'm just about ready to go home; it's so hot here."

They didn't notice the three men who were sitting on a bench close by. When the men heard them mention elureum and Qumarians, their ears perked up. The kids didn't know it, but these men were part of the group of Qumarians who were there to get the elureum, and now they knew what Mohammed was planning to do.

One of them immediately took out his cell phone and dialed. "Polari, this is Mishcan. I have some bad news for you."

CHAPTER 12
(اثني عشر)
~ <u>ith</u>-nah ah-<u>shar</u> ~

"We are in the park near the zoo and just heard some American kids say that Mohammed is going to call the police to arrest us after we get the elureum," explained Mishcan.

"What?!" said Polari. "That's impossible!"

"It sounds impossible to us too, but we just heard them say it."

"Get those kids and bring them to me right away," Polari shouted.

Mishcan and his two partners, Yedi and

Siimi, rushed down the street to find the kids. They saw them turn into the zoo entrance and entered behind them.

Once inside, they followed the crew's every move, staying far enough away to not be noticed.

The kids walked around the small zoo, seeing giraffes, elephants, cheetahs, lions, tigers, zebras, and lots of other animals they recognized. They sat in on an animal show with trained dogs that was a lot of fun. The trainer invited Kian to come up on the stage and be a part of the show, and he loved it. The kids were afraid he might try one of his magic tricks, which would have totally embarrassed them, but fortunately, he didn't.

When the show was finished, Kian ran back into the audience and reminded his friends, "The stage is my home; soon you'll see me performing on one every night."

They laughed and hoped he was right.

Walking out of the animal theater, they

passed three men standing near the exit.

"Have you noticed those guys hanging around us?" asked Kian.

"Yeah, I saw them earlier but didn't think much about it," said Nikko.

"I think they're up to something. Let's get away from them," said Kian.

They took off running, and the men followed. They ran as fast as they could, but the men were catching up. Suddenly, Eddie saw a zoo guard and hurried over. The others weren't sure if they should follow, but Eddie was obviously up to something and his crazy ideas usually worked out well.

"Can you help us, please?" said Eddie, crying big crocodile tears. The other kids caught on and started crying too.

"We got lost from our school group and don't know what to do," Eddie continued between tears.

"I'm sorry, boy. Come with me. I will help you," the guard said as he put his arm around

Eddie and walked him over to the guard station, while the others followed.

The guard made an announcement over the loudspeaker that some children were lost. He made it again and nobody answered. Finally, he decided to take them to the zoo's central office to see if someone could help him locate the rest of the school group.

The men followed, careful not to get too close.

The kids waited and waited with the guard in the office, but, of course, no one came to retrieve them.

"I'll call the teacher," said Gold, pulling out her cell phone and pretending to dial. She spoke as though there was someone on the other line. When she hung up, she told the guard, "One of the vans broke down, so they left with half of the kids and are coming back to get us."

"OK, just relax and have something to drink,"

said the guard.

After about ten minutes, Gold made another call.

"They're at the back entrance. Can you take us there?"

"Of course, let's go."

They walked with the guard to the gate, and the three men followed from a distance. When they reached the door, Gold said, "There's the school bus, come on guys, let's go."

Once outside, all five kids took off running. The guard was confused and didn't understand what was going on. He walked back into the zoo, shaking his head.

The kids had escaped the men, but wondered who they were, and why they were chasing them.

Arriving at the boulevard, they hailed a taxi and jumped in.

"How much to go to Tahrir Square?" Kian asked. They knew the square was a big area in the center of town, and it would be easy to get lost there if they needed to.

"Eight pounds," said the driver.

"And how much for air conditioning?" asked Nikko, winking at his friends.

"Ha ha," said the driver. "You're smart. It's five pounds more."

"That's too much," said Nikko. "We'll pay three."

"OK, three is good," said the driver, and they took off.

When they arrived, they ran inside a video game store and mixed in with the crowd. It would be difficult to find them there. They were still wearing the white clothing that Amman had given them earlier, so they blended in with the Egyptians.

They stood in a corner, and Nikko said, "I don't know who those guys were, but they seemed out to get us. I wonder why?"

"It must have something to do with

Mohammed and the Qumarians. Nobody else even knows we're here. We should call Mohammed and let him know what happened. If we're in danger, he may be too," said Cassie.

"I remember seeing them in the park," said Nikko. "Maybe we said something that let them know what was going on? Maybe they're part of the group of thieves."

Gold called Mohammed but he didn't answer. She had to make a decision.

"Since we can't reach Mohammed, we need to get to the Saqqara Pyramids. He may be in trouble and not know it," she said.

Nikko put Saqqara Pyramids into the navigational system on his phone, and it said it was only nineteen miles from town.

"We aren't far from the Giza Pyramids. Let's go there and maybe Amman can help us get to Saqqara," he said.

They ran outside and hailed a taxi to take

Evil in Egypt

them to the Giza Pyramids. When they arrived, they ran over to Amman's stable, but he wasn't there. They saw Abdul, his other brother.

"Hi Abdul, remember us?" asked Eddie.

"Yes, I remember you. What do you want?" said Abdul.

"Where is Amman?" asked Eddie.

"He isn't here, and I'm in charge of the stable. What do you want?"

Now wasn't the time to play games. They had to get to Saqqara right away.

"Abdul, there is something I have to tell you," said Gold. She didn't want to embarrass Mohammed in front of his little brother, but if she didn't, Mohammed might be hurt by the Qumarians.

Gold explained everything to Abdul, and he wasn't surprised.

"I knew something was going on, but I didn't know what it was. My brother is a good man, but if he thought he could help the people of Qumar and our mother, I can totally understand. What do we need to do?"

"We need to get to Saqqara as quickly as possible. Can you help us?" said Gold.

"Yes, I can. We can get there by camel in less than an hour. I only have three camels, but I have lots of friends here. I will find three more. Just give me a few minutes."

Abdul went around to the other stables and within minutes, he returned with three more camels.

"You have on the right clothes. I will leave the park alone and once I'm outside; you follow slowly. If we leave together, it might arouse suspicion."

"OK," said Eddie.

Abdul rode toward the exit. The kids kept their eyes glued on him. As soon as he was safely out of the park, they followed. Once outside the gate, they took off in the direction of Saqqara . . . six camels on a mission.

CHAPTER 13
(ثلاثة عشر)
~ <u>tha</u>-la-thah ah-<u>shar</u> ~

Riding through the city was a feast for the eyes. They saw elaborately designed mosques where people prayed five times a day and expensive hotels, golf courses, museums, bazaars, bars, restaurants, and nightclubs.

"There's a Pizza Hut!" said Kian.

"What?" Nikko said with a laugh.

"I also see McDonalds and Burger King!" said Kian.

They felt like they were at home with all the

fast-food restaurants they rode past. They even saw The Colonel on one of the small streets. Many of the cars played Egyptian music on their radios; others blasted heavy metal, hip hop, and R&B. Bicycles were everywhere, and the cyclists weaved between the cars, trucks, buses, and camels.

"Are we in Cairo or New York?" joked Gold.

Abdul laughed and said, "We have just about everything here that you have in America."

"I know," said Gold. "We're seeing it for ourselves."

As they neared the outskirts of town, they passed sheepherders calmy walking through traffic with fifty or more animals, and motorcycles swerving between cars at high speeds. In the nearby desert, there were rock formations that looked like animals, beehives, and even an erupting volcano.

"Is that the Nile?" asked Eddie.

"Yes, it is," said Abdul. "And those boats with red sails are called feluccas. Tourists ride them down the Nile with every comfort you can imagine."

The kids looked at the feluccas and saw groups of people enjoying music, cocktails, and laughter while relaxing on luxurious, colorful couches.

"Maybe we can ride one of those before we leave. That would be so cool," said Kian.

"We'll try to make that happen," said Abdul.

They rode another ten minutes and saw three pyramids in the distance.

"That is Saqqara," said Abdul. "And those are the Step, Bent, and Red Pyramids. They were the very first pyramids built in Egypt. A lot of discoveries have been made in this area, and fifty-two burial sites were identified in just the last couple of years. This is where my brother Mohammed works. He and his team are excavating the tomb of Wahtee, a pharaoh from the Fifth Dynasty. They discovered his tomb about five years ago and are

Evil in Egypt

now bringing many of the treasures to the surface to be transported to their new homes. Several of them will be on display in the new Egyptian Grand Museum."

"Abdul, I think I see Mohammed," said Gold, pointing toward the tombs.

"Yes, that is him," said Abdul. "He is my big brother and he would feel awful if he thought I knew what was going on. I will wait here for you and keep my eyes open for the Qumarians."

The kids took off toward Mohammed, while Abdul stayed behind. Mohammed looked up and saw them arriving.

"What are you doing here?" he asked.

"We tried calling to tell you the Qumarians know about your plan to call the police, and they may try to harm you. Coming here was the only other thing we could do when you didn't answer."

"How could they know of my plan?" asked Mohammed.

"We're not sure, but we think they may have heard us talking about it at the park near the zoo," said Kian.

"Did you call the police to let them know the Qumarians would be at the Step Pyramid?" asked Nikko.

"Yes, I did, but no one has come yet. By now, the Qumarians should have taken the package of fake elureum I left at the Step Pyramid," said Mohammed with a smile.

"The fake elureum?" said Nikko.

"Yes, after you told me what they were up to, I got some rocks, spray-painted them the same color as the elureum, and left them for the Qumarians. It's unfortunate the police didn't come, but there's still time for them to get here and arrest them."

Just then, Mohammed and the kids heard the clack of camels' hooves and worried the thieves might be approaching. Mohammed gestured for them all to hide inside the tomb.

As the Qumarians were heading back to Cairo, they noticed six camels outside a tomb. They had already retrieved the elureum from the Step Pyramid but wondered if there may be more treasures inside this burial place. There were no guards around, so they cautiously went inside to see what they could find.

As they entered the tomb, the sun disappeared, and they found themselves in darkness. They walked further into the dark tomb, but the pathway ended just a few hundred feet from the entrance. They tried pushing the walls to see if they would open, but nothing budged.

Yedi stepped on a square of sand on the floor and felt it move. He and the others swept away the sand from the top of the square and a small door was revealed. They opened it and climbed down the ladder propped against the wall. Inside, they continued along another passageway and discovered three chambers. Light reflected on the walls inside one of the chambers, and when they entered, they saw mounds and mounds of precious metals, gold, and silver. There were thousands of pieces of jewelry in each chamber and the reflections lit the rooms like sunbeams. The Qumarians began to think this find might be more important to them than the elureum. After all, the elureum was to help the defense department, but if they could take home some of these jewels, they would become millionaires overnight. They began filling their pockets, bags, and even their underwear with jewels, then they climbed the ladder back to the top. When they exited, the passageway was as black as night.

"What's going on?" said Polari. "Where is the door?"

"It's right here," said Siimi. "But I can't open it. How are we going to get out of here?!"

All four men started screaming for someone to let them out. Outside the tomb, Mohammed and the CLUB US crew heard them, but wouldn't open the door.

"I'll go to the police department when we return to Cairo to let them know they are here," said Mohammed. "I think they're going to have a nice evening inside the tomb."

The kids laughed.

"It's getting dark. Do you want to return to Cairo tonight or sleep here in one of the tombs?" asked Mohammed.

"No way!" said Cassie. "Let's get out of here now!"

Mohammed laughed and turned his camel toward Cairo. As he did, he looked at the kids' camels more closely and said, "Hey! Those are our camels; how did you get them?"

"I helped them, brother," said Abdul as he rode out from behind the tombs.

Mohammed was horrified that his brother knew what he had been planning to do. He lowered his head and didn't say a word.

Abdul steered his camel closer to Mohammed's and said, "Brother, I understand why you did it. I would have done the same. You thought you were saving lives and earning money to help with Mother's treatments. How were you to know what they were planning? You are not to blame."

The brothers hugged and Abdul said, "I love you, brother."

"I love you too," said Mohammed. "I didn't know what else to do, and I thank you for understanding."

Just then, they heard the creak of the tomb door opening. They turned and saw the Qumarians walking out.

CHAPTER 14
(أربعة عشرة)
~ ar-<u>ba</u>-ah ah-<u>shar</u> ~

The four Qumarians grabbed Mohammed and Abdul by the arms and pulled them over to the tomb entrance before pushing them inside and closing the heavy door. To make sure the group would not escape as easily as they had been able to—by using their combined strength to push the door open—the thieves secured the entrance with boulders that lay nearby.

"What do we do about these kids?" asked Mishcan.

"We will take them with us. If we run into any problems, we can use them as hostages."

They directed each of the children to mount one of the camels they had ridden to the desert. They slapped the remaining two on their backsides and they ran away.

"Now there is no evidence that anyone was here. We will get out of the country tonight, with the elureum for our government and the treasures we found in the tomb for ourselves. With it, our lives will be completely changed. We will gain the respect and admiration of our people, and our families will live like kings and queens forever," said Polari.

"But how will we get the jewels past airport security?" asked Siimi.

"We will hide them in the secret compartments in our luggage."

"And if security discovers the jewels? They won't allow us to leave the country," said Yedi.

Evil in Egypt

"When we get to the airport, we will pick the pockets of four male passengers and replace their tickets with ours. If the security guards find the jewels, these men will be the ones arrested," said Polari.

"You're brilliant, Polari. Let's do it!"

"Mishcan and I will ride in front of the kids, and Yedi and Siimi will bring up the rear. This way they can't escape," said Polari.

The kids were terrified. Mohammed and Abdul were locked inside a tomb. They were now hostages, and only hours remained until B.O.R.T.R.O.N. would return to take them home. The crew had never been so afraid that a mission would fail.

As they headed back to Cairo, the Qumarians whipped their camels to go as fast as possible. The kids' animals mimicked their speed. It was nighttime and the route was illuminated by the moon and stars. The kids were all thinking about how to get away from the thieves once they reached the city.

As they approached Cairo, colorful light beams crisscrossed the sky. The kids realized the beams were coming from the area around the Great Pyramid and the Sphinx. They continued and soon heard a thunderous voice that appeared to be coming from the sky. The voice was recounting the history of Egypt and the pyramids while hundreds of tourists watched the light and sound show from the ground.

Without any warning, the kids' camels took a sharp right and galloped toward the pyramids.

"Where are they going?" yelled Eddie.

"It looks like they're heading back to Abdul's stable," replied Gold.

The crew members held on tight. The Qumarians were right on their heels, and when the camels stopped, Polari said, "We have a 10:00 flight and must collect our luggage, hide the jewels, and get to the airport. Let's get out of here; we only have one hour. It's not worth chasing these kids."

They pulled the reins of their camels to the right and sped to the exit.

The other stable owners came running over to find out what was going on. The friends who had loaned Abdul their camels, quickly grabbed them.

"Where is Abdul?" asked one of the men.

The kids were silent. They couldn't tell them what had happened, but they needed to tell someone.

"We don't know where Abdul is," said Gold. "He left us, and the men we were with helped us get back here."

"We'll leave his camels with you. I'm sure he'll be back soon," said Cassie.

The other camel owners didn't know whether or not to believe them but grabben the reigns of Abdul's camels and tied them up at his stable. The kids took off running toward the boulevard.

"What do we do now?" asked Cassie.

"Should we go to their home and tell their mom?" asked Kian.

"No, we can't do that. She will be full of worry. We'll have to think of something else," said Gold. "I think we should go to the police and tell them what happened."

"The police? Are you sure?" asked Nikko.

"I think it's the only solution," said Gold. "We have to save Mohammed and Abdul."

They grabbed a taxi and told the driver to take them to the police station. Within minutes they arrived. They pushed Eddie to the front of the group to speak to the sergeant.

He spoke into his translator, then went to the desk and said, "Nahnu behagatun lilmusaadah," (نحن بحاجة للمساعدة) through teary eyes.

The sergeant didn't understand, so he blurted, "We need help!"

"OK," responded the sergeant with concern, "what do you need?"

"Our friends have been locked inside a tomb at Saqqara. The Qumarians have stolen the jewels and treasures, and we don't know what to do!"

CHAPTER 15
(خمسة عشر)
~ <u>kham</u>-sah ah-<u>shar</u> ~

The kids quickly found themselves in the chief of police's office, along with several other officers. Everyone stared at them with curiosity.

"So, tell me what's going on," began the chief.

"Four Qumarians who have stolen jewelry and treasures from a tomb at Saqqara have locked our friends inside the burial place. Please help us save them!" said Eddie.

"Slow down, slow down," said the chief.

Evil in Egypt

"Who are your friends? How do you know this about the Qumarians and what jewelry and treasures are you talking about?"

Within minutes, Gold had explained everything. The officers stared at the kids, their mouths open. Some smiled because they thought it was a joke. Others looked around, wondering if someone had put them up to it. The chief pointed toward the door, and a group of officers went outside to see if there were any suspicious characters lurking around.

"So, you're telling me these Qumarians have stolen jewels and other treasures from the tomb and are taking them out of the country tonight?" repeated the chief.

"Yes, that's exactly what I'm telling you," said Gold. "And they have locked our friends inside the tomb!"

"Who are you, and how do you know all this?" asked one of the officers.

"We are here from California with our school. Mohammed and Abdul took our group on a field trip to see the Saqqara tombs," said Eddie.

"Who are Mohammed and Abdul?" asked the chief.

"Mohammed is the head of the archaeological team that is excavating the tomb, and the robbers must have known he would have access," said Nikko.

"Dr. Mohammed Yusef? Is that who you're talking about?" asked the chief.

"Yes," said Cassie. "Dr. Yusef. We had lunch with his family as a part of our school program, and they offered to take us to Saqqara."

"My God," said the chief. "We must do something immediately. Grab a car and take these kids out to the tomb to help Dr. Yusef and his brother. Be sure to put tools in your trunk just in case."

"But what about the thieves?" said Gold. "If

you don't catch them, they'll be out of the country soon."

"She's right," said the chief. "Three of you kids go with my officers to the airport to help identify them, and the other two go to the tomb."

They all ran outside where two police vans were waiting. Cassie and Kian jumped into the first van, and headed to the tomb, while Gold, Eddie, and Nikko went to the airport. Both vans took off at high speeds with their sirens blaring.

"This is cool," said Eddie. "We're used to being chased by the police, but it's nice to be on their side for a change."

"The Qumarians have a flight at ten o'clock, so we need to go to the terminal it leaves from ASAP," said Gold.

"Got it," said the officer as he sped toward the airport.

They arrived within minutes, jumped out of the van, and entered the main check-in area.

"Do you remember what they looked like?" asked one of the officers.

"We sure do," said Eddie, searching the waiting room with his eyes.

They walked around the room looking for the Qumarians, but before they could spot them, the men saw the kids and police officers.

"Split up!" Polari ordered.

They all hurried in different directions. Yedi went into a restaurant and ordered a cup of tea. He thought he could blend in with other travelers, but before he even sat down, Eddie yelled, "There's one of them!"

Yedi tried to run, but one of the officers grabbed and handcuffed him.

"I see one!" Nikko yelled, pointing at Siimi. "He's on the escalator!"

Nikko and the officer ran up the escalator behind him, but Siimi jumped across the divider and flew down the other side.

Eddie was waiting at the bottom, and just as the Qumarian reached the last step, he put his foot out and tripped him. A passenger helped Eddie hold the thief down until a police officer came over and handcuffed him.

The crew continued searching the airport and saw a porter carrying luggage with passengers following behind.

"I think that's one of them," said Gold, pointing at the porter.

It was Mishcan. He had stolen a porter's hat and grabbed a luggage cart to disguise himself. As soon as he saw the kids and police coming his way, he ran toward the security checkpoint and jumped over. Big mistake. There were several agents there checking luggage and they detained him immediately. The officers didn't even have to follow.

"The only one left is Polari, the head of the team," said Gold.

They walked through the entire airport but didn't see him anywhere. They went outside where people were arriving in their cars, and there was no one that the kids recognized. Just as they were walking back into the terminal, Nikko saw a strange-looking woman hailing a taxi.

"Officer," he said, "look at that lady. She looks weird. I think she has a mustache, and it looks like she's wearing men's shoes."

They walked over to the taxi stand, and when the woman saw them coming, she took off running. Her hat flew off, and Nikko recognized "her" as Polari, the head of the Qumarian thieves.

"Stop, stop!" ordered the officer. The thief kept running.

Polari dashed across the street and into a parking garage, with the kids and police officers on his trail.

As he boarded the elevator, one officer said, "I'll take the stairs to the first floor and you guys go to the second and third and we'll see if we can catch him."

Gold and Eddie headed up the stairs toward the third floor. Nikko stopped at the second floor and the officer went to the first floor, just above the ground level.

The elevator door didn't open on the first floor, so the officer continued to the second. It didn't open at the second floor, so they all ran to the third. Just as they arrived, they saw Polari weaving between parked cars. They all ran after him, and finally cornered the thief. His only option was to raise his hands in surrender.

The officer handcuffed him and they walked back to the elevator. Gold and Eddie stared at him with piercing eyes.

"I hope Mohammed and Abdul are OK. If not, you're going to regret it," Nikko said to the man.

CHAPTER 16
(السادس عشر)
~ <u>seh</u>-tah ah-<u>shar</u> ~

The road to Saqqara was empty, and the officer raced to the tomb. When they arrived, it was totally dark. The only light by which to navigate was the moon.

The mountainside was nearly a mile long and at night, all the tomb entrances looked the same.

"I can't tell which was the tomb they locked Mohammed and Abdul in; they all look alike," said Cassie.

They walked along the mountainside to see

if either of them could remember anything at all. It was impossible. There were rocks, boulders, and sand everywhere, but nothing stood out.

"I wonder if this might be a clue," said Kian holding up a wide brush.

"This brush is often used to remove sand from objects in the desert for examination," said one of the officers.

"Since Mohammed is an archaeologist, he may have had one with him! He could have dropped it as he was being shoved into the tomb," said Kian.

"Or," said Cassie. "Maybe he left it as a clue in case anyone came looking for them."

"The boulders!" shouted Kian. "Remember they rolled big boulders in front of the door before we left? Here they are! The other tombs don't have them, so I think this might be the one."

Just then the police officer held his finger over his lips and whispered, "Shhh!" He leaned closer to the door as he thought he had heard a faint voice coming from inside.

Everyone was silent. Then they heard a voice that sounded like someone in trouble.

"It's a signal, I'm sure of it!" said Cassie.

They all gathered at the front of the tomb and began pushing the enormous boulders away. Then they pulled on the door until it opened slightly. They were able to squeeze through the opening and enter the main passageway.

"Cool," said Kian.

"This is awesome," said Cassie.

Both walls of the narrow passageway were filled with hieroglyphics and statues of people. As they walked, the kids' eyes darted from one treasure to another in amazement.

"This is very customary in Egyptian tombs," said an officer. "The pharaohs and queens spent many years preparing for their final journey and always documented their story in hieroglyphics.

Evil in Egypt

I'm not an expert, but it appears to be a family tomb. I see statues of children and adults, which leads me to believe they were all buried here."

"Really?" said Kian in a whisper. Being in the tomb was scary, but exciting. He was seeing something he had never imagined or seen before, not even in his schoolbooks.

"But where are Mohammed and Abdul, and where did the voice we heard come from?" asked Cassie.

They looked down to see an opening in the floor with a light shining from inside. Bending for a closer look, they saw a ladder that provided access to a narrow shaft. They descended, one by one, and as they did, the voice they'd heard earlier grew louder. They turned left and continued down a dark passageway with open doors to three chambers. Just past the third chamber was a hole in the wall and from inside they heard Mohammed say, "Alhamd lilah." (الحمد لله)

"What does that mean?" Cassie asked the officer.

"Thanks be to God," he responded.

CHAPTER 17
(سبعة عشر)
~ <u>saa</u>-bah ah-<u>shar</u> ~

When the crew and police officers arrived at the station with the Qumarian thieves and their luggage, an investigator slit open the inside lining of their suitcases and discovered the haul they had planned to take out of Egypt. There were millions of dollars of jewels and precious metals from the Fifth Dynasty inside.

There wasn't anything the thieves could say. They had been caught red-handed, and now could only hope their government would save them.

They were allowed to make one phone call, so they made it to the person who had sent them on the mission.

"Hello," answered a voice on the other end.

"Hello, this is Polari. I am at the police station in Cairo."

The phone went dead, and Polari knew what that meant. They were on their own.

"We have families at home that need us," pleaded Mishcan.

"Well, there's a good change they will never see you again," said the police chief as he waved for the officers to take them to jail cells.

~ ~ ~

Back at the tomb, Kian, Cassie, and the police officers removed the fallen debris that had trapped Mohammed and Abdul. They finally were able to remove enough to allow the brothers to escape.

"Shukran, shukran," they both said with smiles of gratitude.

"Why are you down here?" asked the officer.

"The Qumarians locked us in and since I work here every day, I know this area of the tomb has the most access to oxygen. I thought it would be better to stay here in the hopes of being discovered. Unfortunately, the wall collapsed once we were inside and we were trapped."

"Let's get outta here," said Kian.

"Yeah, it's getting claustrophobic," said Cassie as she turned to head back to the entrance.

Just as she grabbed the sides of the ladder to climb up, it broke away from its anchor and collapsed in pieces inside the shaft.

Now they were all trapped inside the tomb.

CHAPTER 18
(الثامنة عشر)
~ tha-maa-<u>nee</u>-ah ah-<u>shar</u>

This was everyone's worse nightmare come true. They had been so close to escaping, and now they worried they might die there. Mohammed's excavation team was not scheduled to return to the site for a week because of the opening of the Egyptian Grand Museum. He took out his cell phone to call his little brother, but inside the tomb, there was no reception. The silence was as thick as mud, and the kids were scared out of their wits.

"We must stay calm," said Mohammed.

Evil in Egypt

"There's no way we can scale a twenty-foot wall and reach the top without the ladder. As I explained, the best area for oxygen is where you found us. Let's go back there and hope Amman will search for us, when we don't come home tonight."

They walked back toward their hiding place and one of the police officers asked Cassie, "Why are you here in Egypt?"

"It's a long story," she answered.

"Too long," said Kian. "Let's just hope our friends were successful in finding the Qumarians at the airport. If so, we have accomplished our mission and can go home!"

Mohammed knew his involvement in the Qumarians' plan had been a big mistake, and he hoped they could be stopped before they left the country. He felt good about the fact that he had given them fake elureum, so no matter what, the people in Borduria would not be harmed as planned. And now that they have been exposed, he was sure the attack wouldn't take place at all.

"I am so hungry; I'm about to faint," said Cassie. As afraid of the tomb as she was, her hunger took over her feelings of fear. "We haven't eaten since lunch at your house, Mohammed."

"We could all use something," said Abdul.

"Check this out," said Kian, pulling out his translator. He opened the drawer holding the special candies and placed the machine in front of the Egyptians.

"I know these look like candies, but they are actually food, good food," he continued. "All you have to do is think of something you'd like to eat, choose a candy that is close to it in color, and when you put it in your mouth, you'll taste the food you were craving."

Mohammed, Abdul, and the police officers stared at Kian. What he was saying sounded wacky.

"Can you repeat that?" asked Abdul.

"Better yet, why don't you think of something

you'd really like to eat right now," said Kian. He gave them a few seconds then said, "Now grab a candy that's the color of what you're craving." The Egyptians all thought about felafel, one of Egypt's favorites, and they each grabbed a brown candy.

"I'm craving a pepperoni pizza with tomato sauce, so I'm taking a red one," said Cassie. "What about you, Kian? What do you feel like eating right now?"

"A cheeseburger of course," he responded. "It's my favorite meal and I haven't had one for a couple of days." He grabbed two candies, one for the burger and one for the cheese.

"Ready?" asked Kian.

The kids smiled, and the adults played along, even though they were still skeptical.

They all popped the candies in their mouths and chewed. Abdul stood up with a look of shock.

"It's felafel!" he exclaimed. Then he tasted tea and looked at his brother, "Koshary tea, unbelievable! You too, brother?"

"Ana aydan!" (أنا أيضا) said Mohammed, nodding his head. "I'm tasting the same thing. "This is crazy!"

They continued eating, drinking, and laughing until, suddenly, Cassie said, "Listen!" Do you hear that?"

Everyone was quiet as the sound of police sirens got louder and louder. Rescue was on the way! They ran into the shaft and waited. Within a few minutes, they heard footsteps in the tomb and yelled, "We're here! Nahnu huna (نحن هنا)!"

Suddenly, familiar faces appeared. Gold, Nikko, and Eddie were peering into the shaft, and two police officers were looking over their shoulders.

"I can't believe you came," said Cassie.

"Now we just need a ladder and we're out of here!" said Kian.

One of the police officers ran to the van and

came back with a collapsible ladder that extended about sixteen feet.

"This is the maximum length I can make it," he said as he lowered the ladder into the shaft and leaned it against the wall. He then took out a rope and tied a double knot every foot or so. "I'm going to lower this rope and you'll be able to climb the remaining four or five feet by grabbing the knots," he said to those waiting at the bottom.

"Now, guys," he said to Eddie, Nikko, and Gold. "We have to hold this end to give them the support they'll need. Think we can do it?"

"I know we can do it!" said Eddie. "C'mon, guys, let's make this happen."

The first police officer grabbed the end of the rope closest to the hole, and the others stood behind him, with the second police officer at the end.

"I'll go first to make sure it's safe," said Mohammed. "Then I can help pull the rest of you up." Mohammed climbed the ladder, and once he reached the top, he grabbed the rope and continued his ascent. The kids and police officers at the top held steady so Mohammed wouldn't slip.

As soon as he stepped foot outside the shaft, everyone cheered and hugged.

Mohammed joined the back of the line to provide support to Abdul and the others. Once they were all out, they ran to the door and exited the tomb. The moon was shining brightly as they ran outside, and the kids all hugged. They were grateful their friends had not given up on them.

"We begged and pleaded with the police chief to send someone to find you, and he finally agreed," said Gold.

"It's a good thing," said Cassie, "because we weren't sure if there was going to be enough oxygen for all of us to survive."

"Alhamd lilah," said Abdul and Mohammed as they hurried to the police van. Though it was crowded, they enjoyed the ride back into town, laughing all the way. Cassie and Kian recounted the fun reaction the Egyptians had to the candies, while the other police officers looked at them in disbelief.

"It's hard to believe my friend, but it's true," said Mohammed.

Soon they saw the spotlights on the Great Pyramids and the Sphinx. Mohammed and Abdul asked the officer to drive them over to the pyramids so they could find their camels. The sound and light show was finished, and all the camel owners were packing up to leave.

"Abdul, your animals are here," said his friend Ghareeb. "Two camels just showed up by themselves and we knew they were yours, so we tied them up with the others and made sure they were well taken care of until you got back."

"Shukran," said Abdul.

The brothers and the five children mounted

the four camels and walked toward the main boulevard to go home. Once again, the camels knew the route. They walked into the backyard and the brothers made sure they were tied up and the lock on the gate was secure. It had been a long, long day and everyone, including the camels, was tired.

The group tiptoed up the steps and entered the house through the kitchen door. The kids saw some of the leftover desserts from lunch and asked if they could eat a few.

"Bialtabe," (بالطبع) said Amman. "Take as many as you want. Where have you been, brothers? I was worried about you."

"It's a long story, little brother, but I'll make it short so we can go to bed. We're all tired, and the kids must leave early."

They told Amman the whole story. It sounded incredible, but he knew they were telling the truth.

"The only thing I don't understand," said

Amman, "is what happened with the elureum. Did the police confiscate that as well?"

"Yes, they did, brother, but they will soon find that the elureum the thieves have is fake. I painted rocks the color of the metal to fool them and it worked. Once the police test it, they will see it isn't real. Unfortunately for the thieves, they stole millions of dollars of historical treasures from the tomb, so they're going to be in real trouble."

"My sons, I am very proud of you," said Mrs. Yusef. She had heard the story and wasn't surprised at the outcome, because she knew her boys always tried to do the right thing. "Your father would have been proud of you, too.

"Now to bed, all of you. I've prepared a comfortable place for the children to sleep, and I'll have breakfast ready for you in the morning."

Mrs. Yusef knew how lucky she was to have sons who would jeopardize their safety to help her, and help others, and she was thankful.

The kids and the Yusef brothers beelined it to bed, and within minutes were sound asleep. It had worked out exactly as planned, and the CLUB US crew could rest knowing they would be home in a couple of hours.

CHAPTER 19
(تسعة عشر)
~ taa-say-<u>ah</u> ah-<u>shar</u> ~

Everyone awoke to the wonderful smells of an Egyptian breakfast. The kids washed their faces and headed to the table. It was six o'clock, so they had time for breakfast and more conversation with the family. Mrs. Yusef's breakfast was just as delicious as her lunch, and they ate until they couldn't take another bite. She showed them lots of family pictures, and Nikko played a game of backgammon with their grandfather. He couldn't beat him, but he had fun trying.

"The only thing we didn't have a chance to do was to ride a felucca down the Nile," said Nikko. "I guess we'll have to save that for our next visit."

It was time to go, so the kids gathered their belongings and thanked the Yusef family for everything they had done for them.

The three brothers and the kids walked to the yard and mounted the camels for the ride back to the pyramids. None of the stables had opened for business yet, so Mohammed, Abdul, and Amman taught the kids some of their camel-riding tricks. Before they knew it, they were doing the same turns and spins, almost as good as the brothers. It was a lot of fun, and they felt like stars in an Egyptian adventure, and they were . . . too bad they were the only ones who would ever see it.

The CLUB US crew still had about twenty minutes before departure, so the kids decided to surprise B.O.R.T.R.O.N. with an early arrival.

Evil in Egypt

They said goodbye to the brothers and gave them each one last hug.

"We will always remember you," said Gold.

Mohammed said, "We will see each other again, God willing."

"Na'am, na'am, na'am," said the kids as they waved goodbye and walked toward the pyramid.

"Where are you going?" asked Amman. "Don't you have to go to the airport?"

"No, we have a special way to return home, and we take off right here," said Gold.

They then waved goodbye and turned the corner.

The brothers looked at each other in confusion. They didn't understand how anyone could take a flight from the pyramid. Their curiosity got the better of them and they followed. When they turned the corner, the kids were climbing the pyramid's stairs and, in the sky, they saw what they thought was a drone.

The drone landed on the step where the kids were standing, and the door opened. It was then they realized it was a miniature spaceship. Even more shocking, the kids stood in a circle on the step of the pyramid, said something that sounded like 'Mission Complete', and started shrinking.

Mohammed, Abdul, and Amman blinked their eyes in disbelief, but what they thought they were imagining was true. The kids were now small enough to enter the spaceship, and the door closed behind them. B.O.R.T.R.O.N. took off and disappeared into the sky, and the brothers stood there, mouths wide open.

"I've seen many wondrous things," said Mohammed, "but this is a first."

CHAPTER 20
(عشرون)
~ **ah-eesh-<u>roo</u>-en** ~

"Bravo," said B.O.R.T.R.O.N. "I'm proud of you. You made it back fifteen minutes early this time! How did everything go?"

"It was amazing," said Eddie. "I still can't believe we were in such an exotic destination and did things like ride camels, explore tombs, and for once, work to help the police instead of running from them."

They all laughed and agreed with Eddie.

"But the best part was meeting the Yusef

family. The three brothers—Amman, Abdul, and Mohammed—were great guys, and their mom was the best cook ever! She even gave each of us a napkin full of breakfast pastries to bring home. I wish you could taste one, B.O.R.T.R.O.N.," said Kian.

"I do too," said B.O.R.T.R.O.N., flashing the lights on the computer screen. "However, it might be a good idea to eat them now. You don't want to risk your parents asking where you got them. After all, I'm sure they are not like any pastries you could buy in Hamilton City."

B.O.R.T.R.O.N. was right, and they devoured the pastries before landing.

Soon they were back home and, as always, they already missed their most recently visited destination.

One day this will be over, thought Nikko with a bit of sadness. *I wish it would never end because being a member of CLUB US is the best thing that's ever happened to me.*

They landed on the desk in Mr. Smith's library, and he and Barks were there to greet them.

"Oh my gosh, Mr. Smith," said Cassie. "This adventure was amazing! I plan to remember every detail for the rest of my life."

"Wow, Cassie, I've never heard you sound so enthusiastic. This must have been a good one."

"It was, Mr. Smith," said Gold. "We have to tell you all about it. You'll never believe what happened."

"I'm sure I will," said Mr. Smith. "How about we go over to Washington Park and relax near the shore for the play-by-play report of your trip?"

"Epic! And Barks and I can play with this Egyptian dog toy I bought him in Cairo."

Gold gave her little brother the eye, and the other kids broke into laughter.

Another successful mission.

CLUB US

Shukran for taking a trip with us to Egypt!
We hope you also enjoyed *Peril in Paris,
Crisis in Cuba* and *Intrigue in Italy* and
will take a sneak peek at our next adventure,
Mayhem in Mexico in the back of this book.

We would also be so grateful if you, or the
adult that bought you this book, would
leave us a review on our Amazon page
so others can see what you thought
about the adventure.
*Just hover the camera of your cell phone over
the QR code below or visit us on Amazon.*
PLEASE DON'T GIVE AWAY THE ENDING!

Thanks again from all of us!
Gold, Nikko, Cassie, Kian, Eddie
Mr. Smith, Barks & B.O.R.T.R.O.N.

LANGUAGE IN EGYPT

Coptic is the oldest indigenous language of Egypt. Written records of its usage date back to 3400 BC. Egyptian Coptic was the most widely spoken language in Egypt until the late seventeenth century AD.

In ancient Egypt, people also used picture words, called hieroglyphics, for written communication. This system began as early as 3000 BC and had thousands of symbols. It could be written in almost any direction, left to right, right to left, or top to bottom. The reader figured out which way to read it by the direction of the symbols. One of the goals in writing hieroglyphics was that the writing would look like art. A single picture symbol could stand for a whole word, called an ideogram, or a sound, called a phonogram. For example, a picture of an eye could mean the word eye or the letter I. Hieroglyphics didn't use any punctuation.

Today, Arabic is spoken by more than 250 million people in twenty-seven countries worldwide. It is written from right to left. For us, books written in Arabic appear to be printed in reverse (starting from what we consider the back, and read to the front); however, we must remember Arabic is older than most languages and has been written that way for more than 1,500 years.

Below is the Arabic alphabet, which consists of twenty-eight letters. All the letters are consonants; there are no vowels. Try copying the alphabet, then see if you can write your name in this ancient language. Remember, start on the right side of the page, and write to the left.

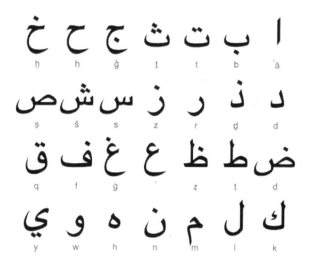

Now trace and then write the sentence below, which says 'Arabic is a fun language'. What side of the page will you start on?

KEEP IN MIND – The diamond shapes over the letters can also be written as dots.

العربية لغة مرحة

Alearabiat lughat mariha.
(*Al ah-ra-bi-a loo-gaht mah-ree-ha*)

Wouldn't it be fun to create your own alphabet using symbols? Give it a try here (or on a separate sheet) and write a sentence to share with a friend or parent.

A-   N-
B-   O-
C-   P-
D-   Q-
E-   R-
F-   S-
G-   T-
H-   U-
I-   V-
J-   W-
K-   X-
L-   Y-
M-   Z-

Glossary

Speaking a foreign language is awesome, though it's important to remember that many sounds in other languages don't exist in English. This phonetic pronunciation guide makes it easy to pronounce words in Arabic, and if you follow the three tips below, you'll soon be speaking the language like a pro!

#1: Pronounce the words in parentheses.

#2: Always put the accent on the syllable that is underlined.

#3: Whenever you see a hyphenated pronunciation, remember it represents just one word.

أبي ، هل تريد ان تأكل؟ Abi Hal toried an ta'akul *(<u>ab</u>-ee hal too-<u>reed</u> an <u>taa</u>-koul)*	Do you want to eat, dad?
عفوا <u>Afwan</u> *(<u>af</u>-wan)*	You're welcome
أهلا Ahlan *(<u>aie</u>-lahn)*	Hi
الحمد لله Alhamd lilah *(al-<u>hahm</u>-du lay-<u>lah</u>)*	Thanks be to God

انا اسمي حسن
Ana aismi Abdul
(<u>ah</u>-na ees-<u>me</u> Ab-<u>dool</u>)

My name is Abdul

أنا أيضا
Ana aydan
(<u>ah</u>-na <u>aye</u>-dahn)

Me too

أراك لاحقا
Arak lahiqan
(ah-<u>rahk</u> lah-hair-<u>kun</u>)

See you later

أرنب
Arnab
(<u>ahr</u>-nahb)

Rabbit

بالطبع
Bialtabe
(bel-<u>tahb</u>)

Of course

هل تعلم این عبدول؟
Hal taelam ayin Abdul?
(hal tah-eh-<u>lahm</u> ah-<u>yeen</u> Ab-<u>dool</u>)

Do you know where Abdul is?

هل تتكلم الانجليزية؟
Hal tatakalam alinglisiyah?
(hal tata-<u>kah</u>-lam al-in-g<u>lee</u>-zee-yah)

Do you speak English?

هيا بنا قم
Hayaa bina
(hi-<u>ya</u> <u>beh</u>-nah)

Let's go

!قف Kef!	Stop!
لا Leh *(leh)*	No
(مع السلامة) Ma alsalama *(mah al-sa-la-ma)*	Goodbye
ماذا تفعل!؟ Madaa tafaāl?! *(ma-dah ta-fah-el ?!)*	What are you doing?!
مرحبًا Marhaban! *(mahr-ha-bun)*	Welcome!
نعم Na'am *(na-am)*	Yes
(نحن هنا) Nahnu huna *(nah-new who-na)*	We're here
نحن بحاجة للمساعدة Nahnu behagatun lilmusaadah *(nah-new bee-haa-ja-toon lil-mo-sa-a-dah)*	We need help
شكرا Shukran *(shoo-krun)*	Thank you

EGYPT

Egypt is located in the northeastern corner of Africa and is one of the oldest civilizations in the world. The country is largely desert and home to welcoming people, many of whom speak English. The Nile River, the longest river in the world (4,135 miles) runs the entire length of Egypt, and many people enjoy a leisure ride down the river in open air feluccas. Cairo is the capitol of Egypt with eighteen million residents, and lots of markets, mosques and museums. The Pyramids of Giza welcome over 5,000 tourists per day and many people ride camels there.

One of the most visited areas of Egypt is the Valley of the Kings in Luxor, at the southern tip of the country. It is where many pharaohs and queens were buried in Ancient Egypt.

Hmmm . . .

1. If you had a chance to visit Egypt, what would be the first thing you would do there?

2. Would you enjoy riding a camel across the desert? Why or why not?

GREAT PYRAMID OF GIZA

The Great Pyramid of Giza is the oldest and largest of the pyramid complex near Cairo. The pyramid was constructed in the 26th century BC and took twenty-seven years to complete. It was built by Egyptians that lived in the area and required a lot of planning. Rock was cut from quarries that were often quite a distance away, and carried on boats on the Nile River to the pyramid location. There were millions of pieces of rock that had to be just the right size to fit. Once all of the stones were in place, the entire pyramid was covered in white limestone and the cap was tipped in gold.

Once the pyramid was completed, armed guards protected it from tomb raiders. If anyone was caught raiding the tomb, they received an instant death sentence.

Hmmm . . .
1. How do you think workers were able to lift the rocks to build the pyramid thousands of years ago?

2. Would you be interested to visit the inside of a pyramid? What do you think you would find there?

THE GREAT SPHINX

The Great Sphinx was built 4,500 years ago to guard the Great Pyramid of Giza. The statue has the head of a pharaoh and the body of a lion. It originally had a braided beard and a nose that some say was shot off in target practice by Turkish soldiers. Archaelogists think the face and body were originally red, the beard was blue, and the headdress was yellow. The structure is 66 feet high, 240 feet long, and 20 feet wide.

Over the next 1,000 years, the Sphinx was covered with sand and only the head could be seen. Legend has it that a young prince named Thutmose fell asleep near the head of the Sphinx, and in a dream was told that if he restored the statue, he would become Pharaoh of Egypt. He did, and later became Pharaoh, just as he was told in the dream.

Hmmm . . .
1. No one really knows what happened to the Great Sphinx's nose. How do you think it disappeared?

2. Draw a picture of the Great Sphinx with the original colors as described above or create your own design.

SAQQARA

Saqqara is an important Egyptian burial ground, and as recently as 2018, fifty-two undiscovered tombs were found there. This site is located only 30 miles south of Cairo and was an important complex of burials for more than 3,000 years. The Step, Red and Bent Pyramids are found in Saqqara, along with dozens more. There are hundreds of tombs in the valley and many have been well maintained. Many of the structures and the lavish internal decorations are nearly as beautiful today, as thet were when originally built.

Saqqara continued to be the choice of tomb and monument builders into Roman times. One later addition at Saqqara was the Serapeum, a temple dedicated to the Greco-Egyptian god Serapis, as a means to promote religious similarity between the two cultures.

Hmmm ...

1. If you were trapped in the tomb with the CLUB US crew, would you remain calm or would you be paralyzed with fear? Which would be most beneficial to the success of the mission?

2. Draw a few hieroglyphics to represent the things you think the pharaohs may have taken into their tombs.

EGYPTIAN GRAND MUSEUM

The Egyptian Grand Museum is located next to the Great Pyramids of Giza and is the largest archaeological museum in the world. At a cost of more than one billion dollars, the museum has 100,000 ancient artifacts on display. And, for the very first time, the full collection (4,549 items) from the tomb of King Tutankhamun is being showcased there. The amount of gold in this collection is mind-boggling and the funeral jewelry is something never seen before. More than a dozen mummies buried for thousands of years have also been unwrapped so visitors can see their faces.

The children's museum is a space for children to learn more about Egypt through games, workshops, virtual galleries, laboratories, and many other educational and cultural activities.

Hmmm . . .
1. What would you most like to see or do in the Egyptian Grand Museum?

2. Which museum in your hometown would you like to show Egyptian kids if given the chance and why?

KING TUTAKHAMUN

King Tutakhamun or King Tut, as we know him, became King of Egypt in 1332 BC, when he was nine years old. He died when he was eighteen. Very little was known about this boy king until 1922 when archaeologist Howard Carter discovered his tomb, the smallest and most valuable one ever found in the Valley of the Kings.

When Carter found his golden coffin, there was another coffin inside, and inside of that one was a third. When they opened it, they found King Tut's body which had been untouched for 3,000 years. There were nearly 5,000 items found in his tomb and it took eight years to remove them all. We may never know the truth about his death, but the treasures in his tomb make him the most famous mummy in the world.

Hmmm . . .
1. King Tut became King of Egypt at age nine. What personality trait do you think was the most important for him to be an effective ruler at such a young age?

2. If you could meet King Tut, what would you ask him?

ANCIENT EGYPTIAN ANIMALS

From the 13th dynasty on, Egyptians had horses, though only the wealthy could afford them. Camels were also domesticated and used for longer desert travel like they are today. Camels can walk very long distances while carrying heavy loads and don't need much water.

The Egyptians were very fond of their pets and they often had cats, ferrets, Vervet monkeys, doves and falcons. Some members of the royal family also had lions and cheetahs as pets. Dogs were used primarily for guarding purposes, however, the favorite pet of the ancient Egyptians was the cat. They thought the cat was a divine or god-like being and when their pet died, the family mourned their death in the same way they would a human, including mummifying them. Cats were so important that it became a crime to kill a cat.

Hmmm . . .
1. What is your favorite animal? Why?

2. If you were allowed to have an exotic animal as a pet, which one would it be? What would you name it?

THE NILE

The Nile begins in the country of Burundi, which is in the middle of Africa, and flows through Sudan, Ethiopia, and Egypt until it empties into the Mediterranean Sea. It is the longest river in the world, longer than the entire width of the United States.

Over 300 species of birds live near the Nile River along with crocodiles, turtles and baboons. Fish are plentiful, and people rely on the river to provide food for their families.

The Nile creates a fertile green valley across the desert. The ancient Egyptians lived and farmed there, using the soil to produce food for themselves and their animals.

The Egyptians also invented paper from the reeds that grew in the Nile.

Hmmm . . .
1. What other uses could a river like the Nile provide?

2. Can you take a guess at how many gallons of water are in the Nile? (answer on the About the Author page)

OUR NEXT adventure
MAYHEM IN MEXICO

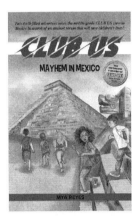

Thousands of children in all areas of Mexico are falling ill from a mysterious illness, and doctors haven't found a cure. B.O.R.T.R.O.N explains that the CLUB US crew must go to the Kukulkán pyramid in Chitchén Itzá and descend to the fourth pyramid underground to find an ancient serum that will save the children's lives.

Thieves also want the serum, and plan to sell it for profit. The crew must beat the thieves to the pyramid, find the serum and turn it over to the officials in order to save the lives of children through the country.

Can they do it?

MAYHEM IN MEXICO

(Excerpt)

Strapping the headlamps around their heads, they entered the dark staircase, with Gold leading the way and Nikko bringing up the rear. As soon as one foot touched the first stair, the headlamps lit up brightly.

At the bottom of the staircase was the entrance into the tunnel. They were expecting to crawl through, but surprisingly, the space was at least seven feet high. The floor of the tunnel was rough, but easy to navigate, and the walls were made of beige-colored rocks. After the first few steps, Gold picked up the pace, and they all sped behind her.

They reached the underground entrance to the El Castillo pyramid and entered. To the right was another staircase, much darker than the first. They walked down slowly and soon arrived at the second pyramid. It was as dark as night in the hallway and even with the headlamps, they weren't sure which direction to follow.

"Let's go this way," said Gold. She turned right into a small hallway and the others followed. As they walked, their headlamps it up the drawings in Maya code on the walls. Though similar to what they saw in the Egyptian tombs, the characters were different. They wished they could read what it said.

"So far, so good," said Kian as they arrived at the third pyramid, but there was one more.

They looked and looked and look for the triangular door to enter the fourth pyramid but saw nothing. They ran they hands slowly along the wall and still didn't see a door.

"Let me take another look at the directions," said Gold. She pulled out the documents from her backpack and read them carefully for the third time. "There's nothing here that precisely tells us how to find the triangular door. We just have to keep feeling the wall for a clue."

"What's this?" said Kian.

Everyone looked his way and saw a narrow space in the wall.

"Maybe if one of us slid through this space there would be something on the other side that could give us a clue about how to find the door," said Cassie.

"That's a good idea. Eddie, you're the smallest, do you think you could fit through that space?" said Kian.

"Sure! Why not?" responded Eddie. Eddie was afraid of taking on this task. But since he was the youngest in the group, he wanted to prove to the rest of the crew that he was willing to do whatever it took to ensure the success of the mission . . . almost.

"What if I get stuck over there and am not able to come back on this side?" he finally said timidly.

"He's right, my mom would kill me if something happened to my little brother," said Gold. "There must be another way."

They continued to feel the walls and suddenly Kian said, "I think I found it."

"Where?" said Eddie, glad there was a better option than sending him through that small space.

"Feel this area of the wall, there seems to be an outline here that looks like a triangle."

When the kids moved their hands over that area of the wall slowly, they felt it. There were two ridges that started at the floor and followed a diagonal path up the wall to form a triangular shape.

"But how are we going to get it open?" said Cassie.

"Let's all push together, maybe that will work," said Gold.

They stood together and pushed as hard as they could and nothing happened. They were at a loss and sat on the floor to think of another way to open it. Just then, the door started opening slowly, with a creaky sound. They jumped up, not knowing how this was happening and worrying they might get captured by one of the pyramid gods. They stood in a corner shaking with fright, when they heard a voice whisper: "The tomb is here, come in."

ABOUT THE AUTHOR

More than anything, Mya Reyes loves being a mom. Her kids have inspired her to imagine fun stories about the amazing adventures they've experienced in their global travels, and CLUB US is the result.

She has visited or lived in 42 countries, worked for the United Nations UNESCO office in Paris, gave birth to and raised Valentina and Mario in Italy, climbed the Great Wall of China, the Leaning Tower of Pisa, and the Giza Pyramids in Egypt.

Mya has a bachelor's degree in French Literature and also speaks Spanish and Italian.

She hopes you'll love reading the CLUB US series as much as she loved writing it!

NILE ANSWER: 680,000 gallons of water flow through the Nile per second!

Made in the USA
Monee, IL
26 January 2022